I0685782

the storyteller
and other tales

by
k.v. johansen

SYBERTOOTH INC
SACKVILLE, NEW BRUNSWICK

Litteris Elegantis Madefimus

First published 2008 by   Sybertooth Inc.
                                                 59 Salem St.
                                                 Sackville, New Brunswick
                                                 E4L 4J6
                                                 Canada
                                                 www.sybertooth.ca

The paper in this edition is acid free and meets all
ANSI standards for archival quality.

Library and Archives Canada Cataloguing in Publication

Johansen, K. V. (Krista V.), 1968-
    The storyteller and other tales: three stories and a prose-poem / by K.V. Johansen.

ISBN 978-0-9739505-8-8

    I. Title.

PS8569.O2676S76 2008   C813'.54   C2008-903531-3

CRITICAL PRAISE FOR THE WORKS OF K.V. JOHANSEN

Treason in Eswy
"The action is fierce and the typical medieval landscape and setting raw and believable. Johansen creates a complex world swirling with mystery, magic, betrayal, political scheming and romance. The reader will settle in for a few hours of gripping the covers until the last word is read..."

— Joan Marshall, *Resource Links*

Nightwalker
"...the fast-paced adventure, compelling characters, and conflicts that make sense will reward readers of this fully realized fantasy..." -*Booklist*

"All I can say is WOW! I've read a fair amount of fantasy/paranormal books, and this is one of the best I've come across. Amazingly well-developed and imagined, both character and story-wise, intelligent, and witty." -*Teens Read Too*

Selected for VOYA's list of the year's Best Science Fiction, Fantasy, and Horror, April 2007; Winner of the 2008 Ann Connor Brimer Prize

Torrie and the Snake-Prince
"Typical of Johansen, the writing fits the world: quest, magic, forests and castles, are all described with rhythm and vocabulary that bring the reader close to this Dark Age fantastical environment....If this book could be compared to a wine one might taste hints of Tolkien, C.S. Lewis, and the Brothers Grimm yet not without sensing the distinct flavour of Johansen."-*David Ward, Resource Links*

Torrie and the Firebird
"Johansen enthrals readers and keeps them entranced....This book is a must-read..." -*Georgie Perigny, Canadian Review of Materials*

Torrie and the Pirate-Queen
"Quirky and original!" -*O.R. Melling, author of The Chronicles of Faerie*

Quests and Kingdoms
"I can think across the years of Marcus Crouch and Sheila Egoff, Neil Philip and Colin Manlove, Jack Zipes and Humphrey Carpenter, and J.R.R. Tolkien himself...all of whom have written interestingly and well about fantasy...Johansen's Quests and Kingdoms is a welcome tradition to this critical tradition." -*Children's Books History Society Newsletter*

"A lively, thoughtful read, and a useful reference volume."

-Terri Windling

taвle of contents

for the c.o.t.p.o.,
which heard these stories first.

FOREWORD

The stories included in this collection were written over a number of years, and take place in a variety of settings. The first two are secondary world fantasies. "The Storyteller" is the most recently-written of the works included here, and sets the stage for a current project, a foretale, if you will. I have always been most interested in writing about people on the edges: the edges of their world, of their society, of humanity. Moth and Mikki, the heroes of "The Storyteller", are two of my favourite characters. "He-Redeems", a different world again, is set in a bronze-age civilisation somewhat modelled on that of ancient Mesopotamia. It spun off from a much longer work, the hero of which is mentioned only in passing, but whose existence precipitates the events of this story.

"The Inexorable Tide" is a tale of Arthur, rooted more in the "historical" tradition of Geoffrey of Monmouth than in the romance cycle of Chrétien de Troyes and Malory, though the pagan Ladies make it very much an Arthur in the modern fantasy tradition as well. The story's most immediate literary influences, however, are Mary Stewart and Rosemary Sutcliff. "The Inexorable Tide" was first published in *Descant* 122, vol. 34, no. 3, fall 2003.

"Anno Domini Nine Hundred and Ninety-One" was inspired by the Old English poem on Maldon, a battle fought by English levies against Norse raiders in 991. The Norse landed on an island, and rather than holding the narrow tidal causeway against them, the local lord, with great regard for the heroic ethos but little tactical sense, gave up this advantage, allowing the Vikings ashore. "AD CMXCI" (then titled "On Þissum Geare") was performed at the Hamilton Public Library by the poet John Ferns and myself in 1994; this is its first appearance in print. The translations from the Anglo-Saxon Chronicle and the Old English

Maldon (interlaced with the text in a contrasting typeface) are my own. Tolkien wrote a play on the aftermath of the battle, "The Homecoming of Beorhtnoth Beorhthelm's Son"; I found my imagination inspired by the thought of the common men involved, who, though they had their own reasons for fighting, perished for their lord's pride.

And finally, a word about pronunciation. The names in "Anno Domini" are Old English; the culture and some of the names in "The Storyteller" are influenced by early medieval Scandinavia and Old Norse; Nimiane, the name if not my conception of the character, is from the French Romance tradition of Arthur but has passed into Modern French and English. Some of the trickier words to the Modern English eye should be read more or less as follows, unless you are a student of medieval languages, in which case feel free to read them as you please! Nimiane > Nim-ee-ayn; Ulfleif > Ulf-lay-eef; Ragnvor > Rahg-n-vor; Hravnmod > Hrav-n-mode; Hrafnsfjall > Hrav-ns-fyall; Pante > Pan-ta; ealdorman > ale-dor-man; Beorhthelm > Bay-orht-helm; Byrhtnoth > Beert-noth; Cerdic > Kair-dich; Cynric > Kin-rich; Aethelred > Eh-thel-red; thegn > thane; geare > ye-ar-ah.

the storyteller

the storyteller and her giant of a man came to the great wooden hall at Ulvsness when the last red light had faded from the roofs. She didn't look to be a skald, butterfly bright to show how lords had rewarded her: no gold at wrist and throat, no scrap of eastern silk. Her undyed tunic was overlarge and rolled up at the sleeves, her dark trousers patched at the knees. Even her long braid was the colour of bleached autumn grass. She was a drab moth of a woman, and, standing in the porch where guests would leave their weapons, that was the name she gave the doorwarden.

"Moth. A storyteller, from far away."

Young Ulfleif reached the porch in time to hear this, and stopped dead in her headlong rush. Something about the stranger prickled her spine. Maybe it was that she had a look of the last queen, the grandmother Ulf barely remembered, who had either defied fate or served some grim foreknowledge to name her Ulfleif, wolf's heir.

Ulfleif was late coming to the hall because she had taken her lyre up to the peak of the Mertynsbeorg to spend an afternoon with the god who had watched the lands about long before the first king, Ulfleif's ancestor, came with his dragon-prowed ships out of the drowned west. The god Mertyn had been in a fey mood, telling Ulfleif, not for the first time that summer, that there were hidden powers come into the land, creeping dangers beyond Mertyn's strength to clearly see or oppose, and that Ulfleif should warn the queen, who never bothered to climb the god's crag. Ragnvor the queen would only laugh at her and tell her that since the death of their uncle, who had been their father's Sword and then Ragnvor's, Ulfleif could not afford to be a little girl, fretting over what-may-bes.

Ulfleif had gotten Mertyn telling tales of the days before the coming of Hravnmod the Wise, stories of demons and gods and the little first folk who still lived on the high fells. They both forgot the warnings, or pretended they had, trying to shape one of the tales into a new song. Why not? Neither of them had the power to escape whatever doom stalked Ulvsness, or the fates that bound them to it. The gods of the high places were born of the land, and watched over it, but they could not direct the affairs of their folk. When the folk chose to ignore them, there was little they could do. Ulfleif, who would have been a skald, was doomed by birth to carry an ill-omened sword, and probably to die in battle, as nearly every man and woman cursed with that sword had.

It made a good story, but she would rather have been the skald chanting it.

Ulf dodged past the strangers, but had to stop to hitch at Kepra as the sword, still too large for her, snagged on the doorpost. She was skilled, for her age, with any other blade, but Kepra thwarted her even in little things. And in her

haste she'd gone and left her lyre on the Mertynsbeorg for
the dew to warp. The doorwarden sniggered. Ulfleif
glanced up, into the storyteller's sea-grey eyes, and froze.
Not a mere chance resemblance in the bones; it was like
staring into her sister's silver mirror. Her own eyes, her
grandmother's — some bastard kin come home?

The storyteller had to see it too. "Who are you?" she
demanded, as though she had every right to make demands
of a princess in her sister's hall. The woman's gaze slid to
Kepra's garnet-studded hilt. Her man touched her shoulder,
reminder of courtesies a storyteller ought to know. She
bowed then.

"I'm called Moth. This is Mikki."

"Ulfleif Reginsdaughter," Ulf said, wondering, Moth
who? Mikki of where? She eyed Mikki, whose head
brushed the lintel of the door. He was an evident foreigner,
with his moon-pale skin and eyes black as sea-coal, though
his unkempt hair and beard were barley-gold. Ulfleif had
taken him for the storyteller's servant, even a bondman,
barefoot and dressed in nothing but an unbelted tunic. That
hand on the shoulder was not a servant's gesture, though,
and it was Moth, not Mikki, who carried the one bundle.

A sword? Wrapped in dark cloth and tucked under her
arm, but it had the length. How had the doorwarden missed
it? Moth gave her the merest shake of the head and a wry
smile that was hardly there, and Ulfleif swallowed her protest unspoken.

"Ulfleif, the Queen's Sword," the hallmaster corrected,
coming to greet the strangers as Ulfleif edged away.

"Ah," the storyteller said, and, as if it answered much,
"The Queen's Sword. With the sword of the Queen's
Sword."

Ulfleif fled, though there was no hint of mockery in
Moth's voice. To be the King's or the Queen's Sword, the
elder sibling's champion, was the second child's doom in

their family, tradition that had come over the sea with
Hravnmod the Wise. It was hardly her fault she came to it
so young, a girl not yet a woman, but they all made a joke
of her — when they did not whisper she was fated, by her
very name, for treachery.

"Your knees are torn," Ragnvor reproved Ulfleif when
she reached the dais. "Were you up to see Mertyn again?
You shouldn't pester the god like that."

"Climbing," said Ulfleif. "Builds muscle."

Ragnvor nodded, barely listening, and turned her attention back to her wizard, handsome, charming, red-haired
Yorthas — who, some muttered, had his mind set on being
more than wizard to the queen. Yorthas gave Ulfleif a sym-
pathetic wink.

"A storyteller's come," Ulfleif offered. Ragnvor nodded
again. Ulfleif sighed. Yorthas was in the low-backed chair
that should be hers by the queen's high seat. Rather than
squeezing onto a lower bench or drawing attention to herself by sending someone for a stool, Ulfleif took bread and
a wooden platter of pork and kale from the table, and
leaned against the wall behind her sister's seat. The place of
the Queen's Sword was watching. She would watch, since
it seemed doorwarden, hallmaster, and even the warriors
who were the queen's hearthswords were failing to do so.
Ulfleif watched as the hallmaster showed Moth and her
man to a seat on the bench along the wall. The fire flared
between them, but she saw Moth watching her in turn. She
knew the woman, deep in the heart, in that place where she
had to bury all the songs, but that did not mean she was
going to completely ignore the fact a stranger had brought a
sword into the hall.

"Oh, sit down," Ragnvor said, noticing Ulfleif's stance.
"I don't expect you to save me from enemies today, little
sister." Ragnvor's own sword leaned on the arm of her
chair, and if any enemies stormed the hall it would be

Ragnvor defending Ulfleif, while the Queen's Sword tripped over Kepra and dropped it on her toe.

Ulfleif shrugged and stayed where she was. Ragnvor laughed and settled back to her meal, sharing her drinking-horn with Yorthas.

The storyteller watched the high table across the flames and Ulfleif frowned at the red glow reflected in her eyes. Her man's flashed green. Ulfleif rubbed her own. Salt drift-wood in the fire. Green and blue danced on the edges of the flames.

While her sister's gleeman sang old songs indifferent well in a cracked voice, never varying from his last rendering, likely not from the one forty years before, Ulfleif amused herself guessing what sort of tales the storyteller brought. Peasant tales, if her clothes were any guide. Cunning shepherds and earthy demons? Her accent was careful and somewhat strange to the ear, but more suited to a lady than a labourer. New romances from the south, full of over-mannered maidens and anguished lovers? She rather thought not. Moth was Northron, even if her tongue would not let Ulfleif name the exact bay or high dale. Old familiar tales of the north with the flavour of some other king's folk, she decided, and prepared to enjoy herself.

When the trestle tables were cleared away and the servants circled with brimming jugs, the hallmaster brought the storyteller forward and gave her name to the queen.

Moth didn't stand formally before the hall, before the queen. She sat herself uninvited on the edge of the long central hearth, that distrusted bundle by her foot. People whispered, even laughed. Peasant manners. But as she spoke — it might have been for the queen alone, or for Ulfleif — her voice reeled all the folk of the hall in to her. The gleeman, skilled in that at least, threw out careful notes from his harp to fall among Moth's words, bright as silver, dark as midnight forest.

But Ulfleif could have chanted the words herself. The merest babe in the hall could.

Long ago, in the days of the first kings in the north, there were seven devils escaped from the cold hells, where the Old Great Gods had sealed them after the great war in the heavens.

And in the days of the first kings in the north, there were seven wizards. These wizards were wise, and powerful. They knew the runes and the secret names, and the patterns of the living world and of the dead. But the seven wizards desired to know yet more, and see yet more, and to live forever like the gods of the high places and the goddesses of the waters and the demons of the forest and the stone and the sand and the grass.

Now the devils, having no place, had no bodies, but were like smoke or like a flame, and not of the earth at all. Some folk even call them kin to the Old Great Gods, though this is heresy —

"Of course," said the storyteller, though which statement her voice mocked, Ulfleif could not decide.

And these seven devils who had escaped the cold hells hungered to be of the stuff of the world, as the gods and the goddesses and the demons of the earth may be at will, and as men and women are whether they will or no. But they did not desire loving worship and the friendship of living men and women, as do the gods of the high places and the goddesses of the waters. They did not watch and judge and cherish the souls of human-folk after death, as the Old Great Gods are said to do —

Was she some philosophical heretic of the far east, to add 'are said to'?

— in the land beyond the stars. The devils craved dominion as the desert craves water, and they knew neither love nor justice nor mercy. They made a bargain with the seven wizards, that they would join their souls to the wiz-

ards' souls, and share the wizards' bodies, sharing knowledge, and unending life, and power.

But —

"So the story goes," Moth added.

— the devils deceived the wizards, and betrayed them. The devils took the souls of the wizards into their own, and become one with them, and devoured them. They walked as wizards among the wizards, and destroyed those who would not obey, or who counselled against their counsel. They desired the homage of kings and the enslavement of the folk, and they were never sated, as the desert is never sated with rain. They would have ruled the earth and the folk of the earth and its gods and its goddesses; they would have devoured the spirit of the living earth and turned the strength of the earth against the Great Gods in their heaven.

So the kings of the north and the tribes of the grass and those wizards whom the devils had not yet slain pretended submission, and plotted in secret, and they rose up against the tyranny of the devils and overthrew them. But the devils were devils, even in human bodies, and not easily slain. Only with the help of the Old Great Gods were they bound, one by one, and imprisoned — in stone, in water, in earth, in the heart of a flame, in the youngest of rivers, in the oldest of trees, in the breath of a burning mountain, as all the stories say. And they were guarded by demons, and goddesses, and gods. And the Old Great Gods withdrew from the world again, to await the souls of human-folk in the heavens beyond the stars.

That preamble should have taken them into one of the many stories of the war of the seven devils, which everyone knew. But the storyteller pulled them into another tale, not one of the usual cycle, weaving new words into the old pattern. Ulfleif, on the first name, shook her head, not wanting to hear again of her namesake's shame and treachery, and warning against telling it here, under this roof where Hravnmod King died betrayed. Moth saw the warning, Ulfleif knew she did, but she went on speaking. Mikki, though, rose and disappeared into the darkness of the porch.

In the days of the first kings in the north, *said the storyteller,* there was a woman named Ulfhild the King's Sword. She was the sister of Hravnmod the Wise, his captain, because her mother had raised her to be so, just as her grandmother had set her feet on the path of wizardry, in her girlhood at Hravnsfjall, Ravensfell in the lost western islands. If her heart yearned for another road and she ran at the heels of her father's skald all her childhood, she knew her duty nonetheless. When the world broke and burned around them and the sea rushed in, it was not her harp she saved, but the sword she had inherited from her uncle, to carry to the founding of the kingdoms in the north.

Ulfhild was one of the seven wizards of the tales. She became the devil Vartu Kingsbane, who was perhaps not the most powerful of the seven devils, but who would be the most hated, for Hravnmod the Wise was a beloved king, and all the tales agree it was she who betrayed and slew him.

Now, in this tale, long years after those days, long years after the stories you know, the devil Vartu, who had once been Ulfhild, the silver wolf of Ulvsness, slept in what might pass for death — swordless, fleshless, but she slept lightly. Death could not take the devils and the Old Great Gods would not. Earth bound her, earth prisoned her, buried deep beneath a grave-hill of tunnels and caves and chambers where the little first folk had once laid the bones of their dead, generation upon generation, turning a natural ridge into a great mound, a village of the dead. A demon of the earth stood sentinel, lest the devil find a way to weaken the bonds the Old Great Gods themselves had set on her.

You all know what is said of the demons: 'Though they may wander all the secret places of the world, their hearts are bound each to their own place.' The grave-hill of the first folk was the place of the great bear-demon Moraig and had been since before bones were ever laid there. Save for her, it was a place of stillness, almost forgotten in the heart of the earth. And there Vartu lay, through season upon season, and none spoke to her but the bear's son.

"The what?" demanded the queen's wizard, and the tale shattered. Even Ragnvor gave him a stern look for his rudeness, but Yorthas only laughed, like a boy. The queen smiled forgiveness. Ulfleif made a face, then realized the storyteller had seen it.

"Ah," said Moth gravely. She drew up her knees and locked her hands around them. "Didn't I say the demon had a son?"

"How?" Yorthas asked, all innocence. He glanced sidelong at Ragnvor and curled his lip at his own mocking cleverness.

"In the usual way," the storyteller said mildly. "She loved a man. A human man, a Northron raider whose heart had turned to peace and the growing of cabbages, who cleared a steading in that distant inland forest and fell in love with a demon's song. She bore a son, and when the sun set on the first day of his life, blind mewling cub turned to naked squalling babe. Which worried her, as you might imagine."

Moth made a place for them to laugh, then, and they were glad to do it, but Yorthas would not let it alone.

"How perverse."

"Do you think?" Moth remained unruffled. "It's a tale. Not one for tonight. Moraig's lover died when old feud caught up with him. The demon avenged him, and mourned, and raised her man-cub in the caverns of the devil's grave. The cub grew and went wandering, driven by his father's

restless blood. He lived among human-folk in lands like ours where demons are not feared. But he always returned to the land of his mother's heart, and when he did, he brought tales of the wide world and told them to the devil, sitting by a cavern where maybe a bone or two showed in the dry earth that sifted between the stone slabs of the roof.

"Why?" Ulfleif whispered it before Yorthas could, and bit her lip, ashamed of discourtesy.

"Perhaps he had grown used to the noisy ways of men," Moth suggested. "Perhaps he found his mother's calm stillness and her sweet sad singing over-lonely. Perhaps he'd thought too long on the stories of the first kings in the north, and laid his own colours over Ulfhild's tale."

The bear's son came often to the devil's grave, as demons judge time. He told of how the first kings in the north, and the seven wizards, and the seven devils, had grown to legend, bright and gleaming and dark as midnight. He told her of travelling among the tribes of the Great Grass and the distant mountains of the east. He told her smaller things, of friends and ships and sea-journeys. He told her of iris and kingcup along the brook, of a thorn-tree in bloom like a drift of snow, of fawns beneath the oaks and beeches, autumn coming early and the geese crying away south.

One time he told her, "They're saying down on the river that a shaman of the Great Grass spoke in a trance with Honey-tongued Ogada, sealed in stone. The goddess of the forest river is troubled; she hears things, feels things, passed between the gods of the high places and the goddesses of the waters. Something is wrong. We feel it, too. Do you? Would you still wake and trouble the heart of Moraig my mother, if you could? Or would you rather sleep till even the stones of the earth have forgotten you?"

The bear's son told her, "I think whatever you gained, you lost more, and I wonder, when I listen to the shadows of shadows of tales ... was what the seven found in the end the thing that you were seeking, or did you lose it on the way?"

Vartu had indeed felt a stirring among the buried devils. Silver threads of power bound her, and amber, and the crimson of blood. Threads knotted and sparked, ran and danced. All seven of them were bound, scattered across the world, and somewhere, one of her fellows had also woken, but not to watch. He picked at the bindings, fretting at the silver threads, until they began to fray. Years had passed, as one, and then another, and another thread thinned. With the weakening of the bonds, Vartu who had been Ulfhild stretched and found faint embers still live in her soul. She shaped, slowly — years, perhaps, passed in the shaping — a rune, and another, and set them on the threads that bound her.

Earth shifted, and shivered, and trickled down the walls of that deepest chamber. A stone fell.

Moraig did nothing, did not sense the runes, or never thought to test herself the work of the Old Great Gods.

The devil drew blood from the marrow, and her bones found flesh again. Earth crumbled, and she dragged a single breath. Then she stopped, and let the bindings lie. There was nothing waiting for her beyond the mound, and Vartu, who would once have turned that emptiness to anger and made the world know that she was free, was only curious, and weary, to find that somehow, sometime, ambition, will, had sunk into ashes.

Maybe it had been when Hravnmod died.

So having nothing else to do, she waited, hidden in earth. She felt, one thread at a time, the slow unpicking of another's chains, weakening the interwoven bonds that held them all, and she wondered what would happen when that one was free.

It was only a tale, Ulfleif reminded herself, a lying-saga spun by an over-bold storyteller for an evening's pleasure, no true history. The devils had been bound by the Old Great Gods themselves.

The threads at which he fretted frayed, spun out to nothing. He was free, Honey-tongued Ogada who had been Heuslar the Cunning. The god of a mountain died, his stones shattering, broken by runes long-laid against him while he thought his prisoner slept.

The web that bound all the seven shivered, weakened, other threads snapping.

If Vartu felt anything, and she was not sure that she did, it was wariness.

Ogada came for her. The first she knew of it was the splintering of trees, the fracturing of earth and stone in a red-skied dawn. Light blinded her, a faint ray spearing eyes that had stared only into darkness since flesh returned to them. The demons, mother and son, attacked, thinking it was some fool come to wake the devil, as wizards talked sometimes of doing, dreaming of a devil bound and obedient to their will. The demons did not realize what they faced until it was too late. Ogada knew the way to kill a demon, even one as great as Moraig. No doubt he had cast runes and searched in dreams; he knew where the demon's heart lay hidden, and it was too late for Vartu to warn Moraig then. Ogada split the oldest of the old oaks with a claw of fire, striking from the sky, and he clove the demon's heart in two with a new-forged sword, Moraig's name cut on its blade in runes of death. Dying, the bear cursed him in the name of the Old Great Gods. But Moraig died nonetheless, and Ogada hurled the bear's son over the brow of the ridge, to fall unheeded amid the broken trees.

Vartu, in the strength of white rage, pulled herself fully into life again and flung stone and earth aside.

"Cousin!" Ogada cried, and tried to embrace her, with no heed for the fine eastern silk he wore or his cloak of slate-blue feathers, though she was filthy, earth-caked, trailing rotten rags.

Vartu pushed him away and turned her back on him to crouch by the great demon's body, clenching her hand in the thick fur, feeling the cooling skin beneath. Kingdoms had cursed and feared and followed her as she looked for something lost, or never possessed, and she had learned to envy a forest demon whose life was the slow breath of spring and leaf-fall, envy a cub who clambered into every muddy hole and hollow he could find, came home burr-tattered and wasp-stung and limping, and went out rambling again.

"Ulfhild ... *Vartu*, you're confused. It's difficult, crawling back to life. It's me, Ogada. You remember me."

She did, indeed.

She spun and kicked the sword from his hand while he gaped, snatched it from the air and swung it, anger kindling a burning wake in the air, but he melted to shadow, a trick he had, and danced away.

"I thought you'd want out of this. Have you turned coward in the end? The Great Gods won't leave us to peace in the grave forever. They'll be back to finish what they began, when they find the courage to face the road from the heavens again."

Earth erupted beneath him, flung him forward, and she hurled the sword like a spear, heard him roar both anger and pain as it struck, but he was gone, fled into the air, a falcon speeding away. The sword fell, its blade shattered.

She had no feather cloak and could not follow.

Demons were not humans, to linger ghostly if left unburied, but she scattered a double handful of earth over the great brown bulk of the bear anyway.

"Go with your heart into the earth that bore you,' she wished Moraig hoarsely, the only parting blessing one could give a demon.

You're still here, the other demon whispered in her mind. Vartu stayed where she was, listening to him, dragging a leg, stumbling, pulling himself uphill, until his breath was hot on her neck and the reek of his blood all around her. He was small only compared to his mother. Vartu would not — she knew that then, and it astonished her — would not, could not, fight this demon.

Even dying, he could break her neck with a lifted paw.

"I did not call Ogada here," she whispered. She had not helped the demon, either. Perhaps she might have broken the last bonds in time, if she had realized that she did care.

"I know." The words were breath as much as voice, felt on the skin.

Vartu looked around, slowly, not to spark a predator's reactions. But the tawny-gold bear only blinked and lowered his muzzle to touch his mother's fur.

"She would say I should stay here, to guard you."

"You can't keep me here now."

"No," he agreed. "I have the heart of my father's people. I'll see Ogada dead. So go, Vartu. Flee. I'll find you again when I'm able." The bear's son licked his mother's face and turned away. Vartu called to him.

He looked back. One side of his head was clotted with blood, and he could barely walk.

"Wait till you've healed, fool."

He ignored that, limped on.

Vartu followed. He endured her following, till he stumbled down the bank at the shallow river's ford and lay panting, unable to rise.

"Fool cub." She slid down after him, took his heavy head unresisting onto her lap, tore her hand with his claw and traced a rune on his forehead in her own blood, then two more, with all her will in them. *Sun*, for life and heart, *boar* for protection, *aurochs* for strength. In silence, he let her, and the sun warmed the both of them. She had forgotten sun, till he told her of it as she lay in her grave. There would be rain before evening; she smelt it on the wind. And so the world went on.

When the bear's son could travel again, they travelled together. Vartu cast the runes and they followed where such foretelling led, hunting Ogada.

But there came a night, a cold night, when frost cracked the very stones and the stars burned sharp and high.

One came, from the Old Great Gods.

The bear's son never woke, but Vartu was called from his arms to stand before a God.

Ulfleif gripped her sword's hilt. Ragnvor drew a breath like she prepared to deal a blow. Yorthas leaned forward, hands on his knees. In all the hall, no-one stirred or coughed or called for the ale-servers. When a log burst and spat a fountain of sparks, they all jumped as though a messenger from the Old Great Gods had thundered divine wrath.

In the final battle, as the devils knew they were defeated, as they went down before the power of men and Gods, they drew on the power of their devils' souls, the stuff of the distant heavens, and they drew on the power of their human souls, children of the Old Great Gods. They drew on the earth of which human-folk were made. Souls of the remote heavens and souls of the earth, they worked one great spell. They set a curse on the road they could not storm, the road to the land of the Old Great Gods. They cursed it, not against the human souls that travel it in death and sometimes return again to new life — their war was never on humankind, though it seemed they had forgotten that, drowning in human thoughts and lost in conquest. The devils cursed the road against the Old Great Gods, to hold them in torment as they travelled it and while they remained on the earth where they had no right to walk.

So though the Great Gods lingered and endured to see the devils bound, they did so wounded and in pain, and their return to the remote heavens was a retreat along that cursed road.

But now, *now* they counted the journey worth the pain it dealt them. Not when Ogada gnawed over long years at the bindings they had set on the devils. Not when he slew a god of the earth and burst his bonds and came to kill the demon Moraig, the heart of the deep woods. But *now*.

The Great God was a stark streak of shifting light, a colour in the air. It came not in battle but to make a bargain.

The bargain was one Vartu could not refuse.

"What was the bargain?" the wizard asked. Ulfleif could have kicked him, though she wanted to know herself. But Moth was patient.

"Her service, as their sword."

"Vartu would have spat in the God's face!"

"She did not. She agreed."

"She never would. Why? They had their quarrels, but she would never betray her fellows. Never. What did the Gods offer?"

"That's no part of this story."

But it is! Ulfleif thought. It must be.

Vartu agreed, and the God withdrew. It would be long ages recovering from its journey in the land beyond the stars. For that, Vartu was glad.

A sword stood in the earth where the Old Great God had hovered, its hilt silver and black niello, its tapering blade obsidian. Already frost settled, white on its edge. Lakkariss. It was made not for battle, but to drink the souls of the seven devils.

Someone in the hall hissed, a breath sharply indrawn. Ulfleif saw the storyteller's man again, leaning in the doorway, a shape too large to be any other.

Moth looked down at her hands, and her voice no longer told the story to each and every one alone. She wanted it over; almost she sounded as though she grew bored with it. "So Vartu cast the runes again, and again they followed, through a year and another, under forest, over water, to the sea-gnawed cliffs of the north and west of the world. They came to the seat of Hravnmod the Wise overlooking the landing-beach that Ulfhild's wizardry had found for him, when they ran before the wind from the drowned islands. They found Heuslar there, her kinsman Heuslar, who was the devil Honey-tongued Ogada."

"And what then?" asked the wizard, sitting back in his chair.

Moth looked up, and it could not be firelight in her eyes; she was between Ulfleif and the fire. "You were a man of honour once, I thought, kinslayer. Maybe it's not entirely the fault of man or devil, what you've become. We all lost our way. I meant to kill you where you sat, but I don't find I can. It seems I haven't quite become a murderer after all."

The giant in the doorway stirred and the storyteller held up a hand, though she could not have seen him. Yarthos seemed to blur a moment, like a fish glimpsed through tumbling water. He rose half to his feet and dropped back into his chair again with a grunt. Ragnvor turned to whisper, "What's wrong?"

Did she not see, had she not been listening? The tale had opened its jaws and swallowed them into its heart. Ulfleif could hardly breathe. And Yarthos, Yarthos flung himself to his feet again, the queen's sword naked in his hand.

Moth still did not rise. "You always did run when the odds were against you, Heuslar, but if you leave here now, you walk out by the door. I fenced the hall with runes against your vanishing. But I give you this, for the man you were — Mikki would kill you for his mother, but mine is an older claim and comes first — I call you to a holmganging, cousin, for my brother. I say before the folk of the hall that once was his and before Mertyn the god of this place, that it was you who murdered Hravnmod and I will prove it on your body in fair fight."

Holmganging was an old thing out of the tales, two warriors on an islet, before fate and the Old Great Gods — though Moth had rather pointedly not named the Great Gods to witness.

"A fair fight?" Yarthos sneered. "With a shard of the cold hells for your blade, as you've had such care to boast? I should have left you to rot and sought out one of the others, someone who hasn't turned coward and bootlicking cur of the Gods."

Moth shrugged, as if she acknowledged the slur to be reasonable. "A fair fight," she repeated. "No wizardry, Heuslar. Steel and blood and human bone. Someone will lend me a sword. And maybe the judgement will be just and we will both die." A glance over her shoulder. "And should that chance, the cub will make certain we both stay dead, this time. He knows what Lakkariss is for."

"Don't be a fool, Moth," the giant in the doorway said, a voice soft and deep as shadows in night.

"Blind! Your brother plotted your murder in the end. You owed Hravnmod nothing. I was trying to save you, to save us and our cause."

"*Hravnmod* might have saved me." She shrugged, letting that pass. "So, you have a sword. Let someone lend me one and we'll take this down to the shore. The tide's out; we can cross to one of the isles at the harbourmouth. No need to wait for daylight."

"Enough of this nonsense." The queen jerked to her feet and closed her hand over the wizard's on the royal sword.

"Give me that, Yarthos. If this is your idea of an evening's entertainment, I can't say I think much of it."

"Ragn! It's not a game!" Ulfleif tried to tug her own blade free, with some vague idea of getting between her sister and the wizard, but as always, cursed Kepra seized on her. Yarthos flung Ragnvor stumbling aside, overturning her chair. Ulfleif yelled as the sword finally answered. She swung, unbalanced, at where the wizard had been, but Yarthos was gone. He cleared the fire in a single leap from the dais. Moth let him pass and only turned to watch.

"I won't fight you," Yarthos snarled over his shoulder. "I remember what's due honour and kinship, Ulfhild, even if you choose not to."

The storyteller's man took one step inside the doorway, the doorwarden's two-handed axe in his grip. His eyes reflected green, like an animal's. He grinned, showing his teeth. Fangs.

"She's offering you more than you deserve," he said. "I'd rather you just died here."

The wizard threw back his head and called fire like a cataract down from the rafters, singing the names of runes. Ulfleif recognized only a few. Someone screamed. Moth quietly drew runes in the ashes on the hearthstones with her forefinger. The fire died and the demon was still there, shaking ashes from his hair, unharmed. Ragnvor whimpered, a sound muffled by her fist, and Ulfleif's hand found her sister's shoulder. Ragnvor scrambled up and Ulfleif drew her back against the wall, pressed close against her side.

"He kissed me, this afternoon," Ragnvor said. "He asked me if I'd ... Ulf, he's one of the *seven devils* ..."

Ulfleif squeezed her sister's hand.

Yarthos' — *Ogada's* body had gone insubstantial as a reflection in water, and within him a column of black smoke roiled and twisted, streaked with livid flame. Claws of smoke struck at the demon and Mikki ducked aside. The doorpost behind him shattered. His axe swept through the devil and trailed smoke at the end of the swing, but Ogada only laughed. Then he was a man again, cut but shallowly, the queen's sword leaping to bite. The axe was faster than the eye and metal shrieked on metal. Ogada danced back, man and fire-edged shadow in one, and men and women scrambled from the benches, pushing their way to the far ends of the hall. None tried to draw a weapon to defend the place, but in the rush old Rolf stumbled on his bad leg and fell. He pulled himself up, cursing, clutching one of the posts of the centre aisle, and it was ill chance the devil found him in the path of his retreat. He swept the old man aside with his left hand, flung him over the fire to land un-moving on the edge of the dais. The wooden pillar was scored half through as if by claws of fire. Red embers smouldered and blossomed into flame.

"Get out!" the hallmaster roared, and contradicted himself. "To the queen!"

Few, even of those who could, did flee out the door. Most could not come to it without crossing where the demon and the devil fought. Some of the hearthswords edged warily around the fire, only to find the storyteller there, between them and the queen. With slow deliberation, watching Ogada and Mikki, Moth unwrapped the bundled cloth from a black scabbard. Frost raised fern-leaves on it. Ferns melted under her hand.

"Out," she said and the warriors scattered. Ulfleif edged forward a little, putting Ragnvor behind her, for what good that would do. Ragnvor stared like a snake-charmed bird and made no move to snatch Kepra from her, which Ulfleif more than half expected, her sister being the true warrior, already the veteran of two battles against summer raiders.

"Did you —" Ulfleif's voice croaked and squeaked when she tried to call to the storyteller — "Did you still want to borrow another sword?"

Moth looked over her shoulder. "No," she said flatly, as the demon and Ogada crashed together. "He's made his choice."

Ogada held the demon pinned to the floor, the queen's sword through an arm. The devil touched his bleeding side, drew a rune against Mikki's chest. With an animal snarl the demon hurled him off and lurched up.

Moth flung the scabbard aside and went straight through the fire. She came out between them, a thing of smoke and ice and churning shadows, with a heart of sullen flame. Mikki stumbled down to one knee behind her, leaning on the haft of the axe. A powerful rune, it had been. With his own blood he smeared it away.

"*Traitor*," Ogada said. "What was your price?" He edged towards the door again. Moth moved with him. The blade was obsidian, as her tale had described. Firelight burned in it; ice edged it.

"Not a question of price," she said, "but of what, in the end, I find worth fighting for. And that is not you or myself or a war the Gods have already won."

Ogada could have fled out the door then, but he charged Moth. The air about him burned. Despite all they had seen, a few of the onlookers shouted encouragement as the devils traded blows, two skilled swordthanes sporting. There was no sporting in their faces, though. They clashed together and stayed. For a moment Ulfleif could see them, two human bodies locked close, eye to eye, sword to sword, two streaks of light pale and cold as the aurora, tendrils of lightning pulling them into one, and then the queen's blade shattered, splinters flying like spears. The black blade struck and Ogada screamed. Ragnvor cowered, covering her ears, screaming herself, and she was far from the only one in the hall to do so.

The obsidian sword drank the light that was the devil Ogada. Light writhed and tore and rushed to the blade as water plunges underground in the sinkhole of a limestone brook, lost to the trackless depths, and the man Heuslar still screamed as if his heart were being ripped apart. Maybe it was. The blade was not a blade, but a vast space, a crack into nightmare, unending fangs of black ice, mountain, crevasse, ice that was stone, under a low pewter sky and a copper sun, cold and sullen. It swallowed Ogada and reached for Moth, who held Heuslar close as an embrace, the sword between them.

Ulfleif tried to move but could not break free of Ragnvor, whose fingers clawed into her wrist. It was the demon who flung himself up and jerked the storyteller away, wrapped his arms tight around her. Heuslar's body fell and the demon, warily, freed one hand to wrench Lakkariss out, never letting go of Moth.

Frost crawled over the blade when Mikki dropped it on the floor.

The burning pillar fell and the beam it supported hung suspended. The whole roof groaned.

"Yorthas!" Ragnvor wailed.

"Get out! Everyone get out!" the hallmaster called, and, "Seize the strangers!" Which was rather less good sense.

Ragnvor still wailed. Ulfleif slapped her. The glazed, staring look left her sister's eye; she made a fist, as though they were back to being squabbling children.

"You're queen — it's for you to command here, not him."

Ragnvor stared, gulped, and nodded, calling to the hallmaster. "Leave them! Just get everyone out!"

There came a sound like a falling tree, a long, drawn-out cracking and a rush of air. Ragnvor pulled Ulfleif back against the wall as the beam and part of the roof plunged into the hearth. Smoke billowed around them.

"Come on. Out." Hand in hand, blinded, choking, Ulfleif and Ragnvor picked a way through jagged abrupt timbers, crawling, clambering. Most of the shouting seemed to come from outside now, but there were still voices within, lost in darkness or trapped at the far end where the roof held. Fire rose up, walling those off. Some of the hearthswords called for the queen.

"I'm here, I'm here!" Ragnvor let go Ulfleif's hand as her warriors surrounded them. "People are trapped in the east end. Cut a way in from outside."

Ulfleif dropped back as they made it to the porch. She turned aside to the dark shape that was the demon, kneeling again, still wrapped around Moth. Mikki spoke, a low, angry-sounding murmur in a language that was almost, but not quite, familiar — ancient poetry given flesh and blood — and Moth once or twice protested. Telling her off, Ulfleif figured, and was suddenly so furious she didn't think before hitting the man on the shoulder with her fist. A bloody arm seized her. Devil and demon surged to their feet. Mikki dropped Ulfleif the next instant.

"Put the fire out!" she yelled at them both. "People are trapped!"

The storyteller stared at her, utter incomprehension; Ulfleif thought that in those eyes she could see all the way down the road that Lakkariss had opened. Vartu was going to devour her soul like the stories said; they would all die in that endless ice.

"Moth," Mikki said gently. "Fire?"

Moth looked around, said, inanely, "Oh," and swept a hand. No runes, no wizard's work. The flame of hearth, roof, pillars, all rushed into the devil's hand and was gone.

It was very dark.

Wood creaked. From the far end of the hall, axes thudded. Someone shouted in triumph.

Ulfleif felt Moth, a movement of cloth and coldness, brush past. Saw an edge of light like moon on snow as she picked up Lakkariss. Moth and the sword disappeared, but Ulfleif heard her, felt her return, weaving and ducking through the fallen timbers. Retrieving the scabbard, she guessed.

"The ridgepole's coming down," Moth said, and gave Ulfleif a shove towards the porch, much as Ragnvor might have done.

the whole roof of the hall did come down, and Moth and Mikki were gone when Ulfleif next looked for them. By the light of braziers and torches, the servants and hearthswords still searched the ruins. Old Rolf was dead, and there were at least four others crushed by falling timbers. Half a dozen injured were carried away to the queen's bower, but they laid the dead out on the clean grass, Heuslar who had for half a year been the queen's friend and counsellor Yorthas well apart. People avoided even walking near his corpse, though Ulfleif supposed the devil Ogada was well and truly dead at last. Or — merely bound again in the cold hells? That, she was not going to ask.

Ulfleif ignored Ragnvor's raised voice demanding to know where she went. She took the path that followed the creek below the foot of the Mertynsbeorg, heading east and inland.

She caught up with grey light promising dawn. Moth waited, standing like a soldier on guard, Lakkariss slung at her shoulder. No sign of Mikki.

"And what does the Queen's Sword want?" the story-teller asked wearily, as Ulfleif panted up.

"Are you just going to leave?"

"Yes."

"What about the hall?"

"Build a new one."

"People died."

"Yes."

"I thought —" Ulfleif began, and stopped. "You should stay."

"Ulvsness already has a Queen's Sword," Moth observed. "And Vartu Kingsbane is not a Sword any queen is likely to want at her back."

"I never wanted to be a swordthane either," Ulfleif confessed. "I was ... I was hoping I could learn some new stories. I mean, you were *born* in the drowned isles. You grew up there. You're the one who *found* Ulvsness! You saw the battle at Vetrgrondal, where the three kings fought!"

"A war my oathbreaking began."

"Oh. Yes. But — I want to know how *this* tale ends."

"I already know." Moth shifted the sword at her shoulder.

Ulfleif persisted. "And you left out — there was no true bargain, was there? What did the Old Great Gods do, to make you carry that sword?"

Moth studied Ulfleif, who knew she ought to be afraid, but could not seem to manage it.

"I ... can't say." Moth looked off, up the mountain, where the pre-dawn grey was spreading. "I'll tell you something I should not, young Ulf, and you can decide if you'll trust a devil's truth. The Old Great Gods are cruel. Not cruel to human-folk, whom they would lock safe from all harm and change in a treasury of souls, if they could. But for the spirits of the earth — the gods of the high places and the goddesses of the waters and the demons of the wild — the Great Gods have no regard, because they have no claim on such souls of the earth and thus count their existence worth nothing at all."

No regard for the souls of the earth ... Ulfleif looked where Moth was looking, up the mountainside. "Mikki? A hostage? Does he know?"

"I hope not. Go away, young Ulf."

"I'm going to." There. She had said it, for her own ears to hear.

Moth was not listening. She looked up the mountain again, and there was the demon, just coming down around the birches, Ulfleif's lyre tucked under an arm.

"Hey, young skald!" he called cheerfully. "I went up to offer our apologies to Mertyn, since Moth won't go anywhere near him, and he said you'd be wanting this. Moth — catch!"

Ulfleif yelped as her precious lyre sailed at them. Moth caught it one-handed; Mikki hauled his ash- and blood-stained tunic off. Mother-naked beneath. Ulfleif dared one admiring look as light ran over the man, before the bear dropped on all fours, shaking his coat into order like a waking dog. He caught the tunic up in his teeth and lumbered on down, limping on a foreleg already healing, demon-swift.

Moth handed the lyre to Ulfleif and tucked the tunic through her belt. "More patching," she muttered, with all a princess's disdain for such matters. But Mikki rested his nose on the storyteller's shoulder a moment and Moth leaned back against him, such an ease and certainty in his being there that Ulfleif envied them both, an envy that was almost pain.

"Are you any good?" Moth asked, with a nod at the lyre.

Ulfleif raised her chin. "Yes." Mertyn said so, and the gods of the earth did not lie. "I'd — I would be a skald if I could. Egill Loremaster of the Geirlingas offered to teach me, if I weren't — I've already learnt the old lays and sagas, all the ones I can."

Moth looked at her with the devil's eyes. Looked right through her, into her soul and out the other side. Ulfleif shivered. Vartu was a thing greater and wilder and more fierce than Mertyn, not of the earth at all. No, Ulfleif was not exactly afraid, only — standing on the edge of something.

"You — take an aunt's advice, young Ulfleif, wolf's heir. Don't burn your heart out doing what you're told is your duty. Don't leave yourself hollow. There are more than enough who can and will wield swords for their queen. Too few to make new songs and carry the old lays into tomorrow."

Mertyn had once said something similar and Ulfleif had protested to the god that she had no choice. She had never considered what no choice meant. Would she go on saying 'no choice' till there truly was none? Whatever Ulfhild had chosen to do in the past, the Great Gods trapped the storyteller now, because she had found something she would not betray. Nothing bound Ulfleif but tradition, and the past stood before her, telling her where that had gone wrong.

Don't leave yourself hollow.

Ulfleif took the sword from her belt. For a moment she held them both, Kepra and the lyre.

"Take it," she said. Her voice shook. She swallowed and tried again. "Ulfhild, take Kepra. It's yours, isn't it?"

Moth blinked, her grey eyes Ulfleif's own once more, sea-grey of the blood of Hravnmod. "It should stay with the Kings' Swords."

"But you'll need a sword," Ulfleif said. "Something other than — than that one." She nodded at Lakkariss. "It's going to be a long road, isn't it?"

Five devils still sleeping. Or not.

Moth said nothing, but she held out both hands and Ulfleif laid Kepra sheathed across them, like a queen gifting her hearthsword. Moth drew it, whispering, from the fleece-lined scabbard. Dawn gilded it.

If Ulfleif did not ask now ... "What does the blade say? The runes I was taught are different from those."

"*Keeper. The Wolf made me for Ravensfell.*" Moth turned the blade. "*Strength. Courage. Wisdom.* Demon-forged in the drowned isles."

"And the hilt?"

Moth ran her thumb over the garnets set in the gold, the hair-thin lines of the runes on the cross-guard. "A prophecy. We never knew what it foretold. The Wolf-smith was a seer and dreamed riddles. It reads, *Until the last road and the last dawn.*"

Ulfleif shivered. Someone walking over one's grave, as the old proverb had it, though how that worked if you had fled the grave, Ulfleif could not guess.

"To the end of the *world?*" she asked.

Moth shrugged, gave that fleeting wry smile. "Probably a charm against rust."

"But it must —" Ulfleif checked her protest when Mikki chortled.

Moth grinned outright, sheathing Kepra. "It's come home. Now *you* go home, Ulfleif. Tell your queen to find a Sword with a heart for it, and get yourself to the hall of the Geirlingas and Egill Loremaster."

"I'll see you again."

"We're going east."

"So might I, someday, after I've learnt all I can here in the north."

"Why?"

"I told you. I want to know how this story ends."

"Too long a road for you," Moth said.

"I could keep you company on it, for a time."

Mikki rested his heavy muzzle atop Ulfleif's head a moment. "Do so, wolfling." He laughed, which shook her to her very bones. "I expect we'll be easy enough to find, wherever we wander. For now, go home, before your sister fears you're eaten."

Ulfleif nodded and turned away, though she headed up the crag. From there, she thought she could watch them going, but mist crept from the creek to swallow them, Ulfhild the King's Sword first, then the bear. Ulfleif struck a chord from the lyre and sang for them anyway.

he-redeems

the three of them lay together on the mat, a single blanket of undyed wool over them. Both the young men had an arm around the girl, and she clung to the one she faced, muffling her sobs against his chest. The other leaned over her, whispering anxiously.

"Don't cry, Barley. Don't. It's not so bad as all that."

"It is, it is. It'll be a girl, I know it, and they'll kill her. I wish it'd never happened. I wish I'd never gone with you. It's wicked. It's wicked, and now I'm the one to be punished."

"Babies aren't punishment," said He-Redeems into her hair. "They're Skarritha's blessing."

"Some blessing," muttered the other man, First-Son. "Not for slaves. Especially not when there's too many girls in the weaving hall already. You ever seen a baby smothered, He-Redeems, and the mother just saying it's the will of the god and *letting* them? You talk about having seen demons when you were with our mistress, but it's things like *that* should give you nightmares. That weaver, Pomegranate-Rain, who had a girl, last month? She never said anything, never cried, just lay there and let the women do it. I was plastering in the next room and the door was open. I saw."

Barley gulped on a sort of shrieking moan, trying still to keep quiet. He-Redeems reached over her to pinch First-Son, all he could manage without sitting up and starting a real fight, which would get all three of them beaten.

"Tell Housekeeper and she'll give you something to lose it," said First-Son. His voice sounded cold, but He-Redeems knew his friend, and felt how tightly he held Barley, how he never left off stroking her hair.

"It's our baby. I don't want to get rid of it. I don't want them to smother her."

"If it's a boy you'll probably get to keep it," He-Redeems said. "Look at First-Son. He was born right here in the palace."

"So was I." Barley gulped a sob. "But they're not keeping girls now. And it'll be a girl, I know it."

"You can't know," First-Son said flatly. "Look, it'd be better if you just confessed to Housekeeper."

"I won't. It's my baby."

"If it's a boy, even if he's sent out to one of the estates, you'd still have him till he was four or five, and he'd still be in the Great Lady's service," He-Redeems said. "Pray for a boy. A son for us, by Skarritha's mercy."

"Pray," said First-Son. It might have been agreement, but it sounded like disgust. "Priest's boy."

He-Redeems ignored that.

"His or mine?" he asked after a bit.

"How should I know?" Barley sniffed and turned over on her back, felt around until she had each by a hand, pressed them over her hipbones and stomach only slightly mounded. Another sniff. "Maybe it'll look like both of you. It could. It's all of ours."

First-Son snorted. "Pray to prevent that, He-Redeems, if you're going to pray. A runty highlander like you."

"With your squint."

Barley giggled weakly, pulled their hands up to her small, high breasts.

She was the first to fall asleep, and First-Son after her. He-Redeems leaned over them to kiss one, then the other. It was good just to lie and listen to them breathing, good to know they were there, an odd sort of family, but family nonetheless.

HE-REDEEMS DIDN'T REMEMBER much from his childhood in the highland village of Rock-Temple, before he came to Korthan. What he did remember was loneliness.

His full name was He-Redeems-His-Father. In the month before he was born, his father lay deathly ill. His mother had made a bargain with the god, that if her man lived, she would dedicate the coming baby to the god's service. His father had recovered, and He-Redeems had from his birth been set aside for great and merciful Skarritha. There had been little love to spare in the household for a child already lost to them. When the time of the Ten-Year Gift came around, and the chosen children were sent to Korthan from all the provinces, He-Redeems was among them, a voluntary Gift-Child, which was rare. Most mothers wept and poured ashes in their hair, mourning the lost child as though he were already dead, despite the honour done them. The Gift-Children were given to be slaves of the god and his Divine Daughter. Some were sent back out to the provinces to work on the estates of the Daughter and of the temples. Others served in the temples. A blessed few were even elevated to the priesthood and to virtual freedom.

Others were chosen in secret rites by the hand of the god himself, to be branded on the chest with the god's sign of the eclipsed sun. They trained to become thonor, the Hounds of Skarritha, the elite soldiers who served the Divine Daughter and through them, the will of the god. The thonor were the bravest, the most loyal, the greatest warriors of Korthan. They hunted out heretics who denied the truth of Skarritha's supreme will. They brought to justice the apostates, who tried to turn back to the malevolent old gods, the nearly-forgotten Nine. And they were in the van when Korthan went to war.

Some of the Gift-Children died on the altars of the public temples, the holiest of sacrifices, to be a pledge to Skarritha of Korthan's continued devotion. He-Redeems remembered the smell of blood and a beautiful woman, beautiful like great Skarritha must have been when he took human form to rule Korthan in the flesh. She was dressed all in gold, with a knife in her hand.

The dedicated children did not cry, and the other children, those who were appointed to be temple-slaves, He-Redeems among them, did not cry. They stood in a cluster just inside the sanctuary where only priests and those belonging to the temple could enter, between the pillars that reached up greater than cedars. They knew the holiness of the place, the sanctity of the rite. They knew they were in the presence of the divine. Or maybe they just did not understand at all. They were very young.

When the next Ten-Year Gift came around, He-Redeems was in disgrace for some misdemeanour and so he had no leave to attend the ceremonies in the temple. He had been down in the cellars moving great wine jars all that month of penitence and celebration; he had discovered then that he was weak, sinful and undeserving of Skarritha's mercy, because in the pit of his stomach he was relieved he would not watch the chosen Gift-Children die.

Mostly what He-Redeems remembered of his boyhood was sweeping the floor of the great temple in Korthan, day after day after day. It was a good life. There was plenty to eat and drink, he was in Skarritha's holy place, night and day, and he was only beaten when he deserved it. He thanked the god, morning and evening, for choosing him for this service, and felt honoured and humbled by it. But when he was thirteen or maybe fourteen, just at the end of that second Gift-Year, he brought wine to the chief of the priests, and stayed to pour it. The holy Divine Daughter of Skarritha was with him.

She was the most beautiful of women. How could she be otherwise, born the near-immortal daughter of a god? Her body was graceful, rounded in smooth curves, her lips full and soft, her skin like honey, and her eyes a darker, richer honey, the kind that leaves a harsh tang of spice on the tongue. The lustrous night-dark fall of her hair was caught up in a golden web with pearls at every golden knot. He-Redeems remembered her from the sacrifice he had seen as a child, and for a moment he smelled the reek of the bowl of blood at the altar's base. His hands shook, fearing that his unworthiness to serve in the presence of such holiness was only too evident. He felt her eyes on him, felt she knew his every secret doubt and fear. But that night, on his mat in the slaves' hall beneath the temple, he knew for certain that he should be damned forever, for the thoughts that came into his head when he closed his eyes. The Divine Daughter was not a woman for the impure dreams of a slave.

The next day he had been sent up to the Divine Daughter's palace, to serve there.

That seemed a lifetime ago now. When the chamberlain took He-Redeems before the Divine Daughter she had asked him his name, as if he were someone who mattered, and had laughed, such a beautiful chiming laugh. She called the traces of the provincial highland accent that still burred his tongue "charming", and praised his manners.

It was not only manners she admired in him. He still remembered the rush of panic, so that his vision glazed red and his ears rang and his knees could barely hold him, when she first reached from her couch and trailed a warm, slow hand down his chest. He thought she mocked his blasphemous desire, and that he was about to die.

"Lie down with me," she had ordered, with her own hands unknotting the cord that belted his plain white gown, and he had done so, lain down, or fallen, drowning in fear and ecstasy and the taste of her perfumed skin.

He-Redeems would never have thought himself handsome, being a short, beardless highlander, but at that time the Daughter had a dozen handsome youths among her slaves — her boys, she called them, who served her in bed as well as out of it — and there he was among them. He never felt worthy of such attention, and was deeply humbled by it. The Great Lady of all Korthan could choose any lord, any priest, any officer she wanted. She did not need to demean herself with slaves. But she was the Great Lady. Nothing she could do would demean her. It was not his place to ponder the meaning of her actions. He had been born to serve Skarritha, the One, the greatest of all gods that ever had been. Service to the god lay in utter obedience to his Daughter, and in that alone.

After a few years the Divine Daughter had lost interest in her boys. She made a captive rebel her lover, a yellow-eyed monster who claimed one of the Nine outcast deities as his mother, and the monster got her with child before he fled the city. It ought to have been a terrible thing, but it was not. She was holy. She could not sin.

that had been during the last dry season. Now it rained, and the Daughter, when she left her bed at all, moved like some overladen raft, slow and heavy.

Barley would grow like that soon, and there would be no hiding it. Poor little Barley, barely done being a child herself. He-Redeems kissed her forehead. Maybe it would look like her, all sharp bones and quick movements like a little bird. No matter who had gotten it, it was their child, part of all three of them, and if it was a boy, maybe it would grow up knowing them and being loved, as he had never been. That was a good thought to go to sleep on.

First-Son, lying with his arm around Barley, his hand pressed between her body and He-Redeems, was breathing deeply and quietly, in time with the girl. He-Redeems let their mingled breathing draw him away. All would be as Skarritha willed.

It was some time later that a gong woke him. He-Redeems sat up, confused and blinking in sudden light with the rest, and asked, "What is it?"

"Don't know," said Barley, rubbing the gummy traces of tears from her face and grabbing his hand. "Where's First-Son?"

"Must have gone out to walk."

First-Son did that when he had trouble sleeping, which happened quite often. He went out and walked around the courtyard, he said, to look at the stars and settle his mind. He never learned to accept things as they came, to trust Skarritha.

Four men held torches high, standing around the chamberlain himself, who was beating the gong.

"Up, up," he called again, as he had been calling for some time.

They got up, some grumbling, some muttering questions of one another, groping for gowns and, the higher house-slaves at least, sandals.

"The Great Lady is brought to bed," the chamberlain announced. "We will assemble in the shrine and pray for her safe delivery."

The whispering grew more animated, and they began shuffling out. He-Redeems hurried Barley through the door between himself and another man. She darted away down the dark corridor to join the women coming from the female slaves' hall. They weren't supposed to bring women into the male hall, but it was often overlooked. Not on a night like tonight, when their prayers were so important.

The slaves' household shrine was a big, bare room, with friezes of Skarritha's life as ruler of Korthan running around the walls. There was no altar for sacrifices, only a statue of the god as woman, looking very like the Divine Daughter, painted in the rich colours of life and dressed in a gown woven of gold. Lamps burned all around her feet, their wavering light making the gown seem to shimmer, as if stirred by the god's breathing.

They prayed, men on the right hand, women on the left, and each in private words. Voices muttered, whispered, broke in sudden impassioned pleading for the Great Lady's safety. She was the Daughter of Skarritha. The god could mean no harm to come to his dearest daughter in this most perilous of passages, but there were ill-willed sorcerers, there was all the hate-filled power of the Nine ... surely the prayers of all her household would be some measure of protection. They prayed, the chamberlain foremost among them at the idol's very feet. When he left to return to his vigil in the Great Lady's apartments, they, in twos and threes, finished their own prayers and went back to their respective halls.

He-Redeems was one of the last slaves to leave. He couldn't sleep, though. He couldn't get the Divine Daughter out of his thoughts. His heart ached for her, not for the Great Lady his mistress but for the woman whose body he had once known, the woman suffering now as woman.

First-Son would say, at least no-one's going to press a rag over *her* baby's face until it turns blue, even if it is a girl.

He hated hearing First-Son's voice like that, shaping his own thoughts. He couldn't think anything that wicked himself. But surely even First-Son would not say anything of the sort, not at such a time.

Eventually He-Redeems dressed again and slipped out to the courtyard, to join First-Son.

the Daughter's palace was a two-storeyed building, surrounding the four sides of a great courtyard. A gallery ran all the way around, patrolled day and night by soldiers, and the flat roof was likewise guarded. There were always sorcerers to fear, and other evil men who did the will of the outcast Nine. A few torches burned on the gallery and the shadows of soldiers moved, but down in the yard, especially under the gallery overhang, it was impossible to see. He-Redeems began to walk, checking each pillar for a huddled, drowsing man. If First-Son had still been walking and fretting, he would surely have heard the stirring within and come to investigate. But a complete circuit of the courtyard did not find First-Son, and He-Redeems squatted down, back against a pillar before the door nearest the slaves' halls, to wait. First-Son could not have left the palace; the only gate was closed and he had no leave to be out, so he was here somewhere, sitting silent and sullen in the dark, perhaps, unreconciled to Barley's state. He would have to come back eventually.

How long he sat He-Redeems was not certain. He dozed off and woke, feeling cold and damp, to the faintly greying sky that promised the dawn. The rents in the clouds were wider and the rain had stopped. He still could not see to the far side of the courtyard, except for the red blur of torches and the blackness of a guard passing before them, but then he did see movement, someone walking quickly from pillar to pillar under the gallery. He thought he recognized First-Son, and stood. The figure ducked out of sight, and then, after a moment, emerged, to come more slowly forward.

"Oh, it's you," said First-Son, when they were close enough to touch. "What are you doing out here?"

"Thinking," said He-Redeems. "Praying."

"You pray as much as a priest."

"Nothing wrong with that. But everyone was praying tonight. Our mistress is in labour."

"Oh," was all First-Son said to that.

"We missed you."

"Who did?" First-Son demanded sharply.

"Barley and I. When we woke up. I couldn't sleep after, so I came out to find you, and I couldn't."

"I went up to the roofs to look at the sky."

"In the rain?"

First-Son shrugged.

"And did that help?"

"No," said First-Son harshly. "It did not."

Away in the shadows of the gallery, He-Redeems thought he saw another figure moving, as quickly and furtively as his friend had, pillar to pillar. For a moment he felt a qualm of fear, that First-Son had slipped from bed to seek out another woman, but a suddenly-flaring torch above flashed on metal, the hilt of a sword high under an arm. It was only a guard.

"We'll go to the shrine to pray again. You'll feel better then."

He-Redeems tugged the man's sleeve, found his hand and led him towards the door. He looked back when First-Son paused to dabble his feet clean in a puddle. The guard was gone; he didn't see where.

In the shrine, a cluster of dancers and musicians prayed on the women's side. First-Son made his own prayers, lips moving silently, and in silence they made their way down the stairs and along the dark corridor to the hall. They found their mat and settled down, comfortably back to back. First-Son fell asleep right away, but now it was He-Redeems who could not sleep. He remembered First-Son stirring the puddle with first one foot, then the other, scuffing the sides of his feet against the uneven bricks as if to scrape off mud.

The palace courtyard was paved in stone and brick. The great plaza that raised the palaces over the city was paved in stone. Only the city streets would, despite their paving and the sweepers, be muddy all the rainy season, with a stinking mix of dirt and dust and dung, and all the rubbish of the households overlooking them.

But there was only the one guarded gate, and First-Son had no leave to be out.

He-Redeems went about his work quietly, taking each lamp from its niche and setting it on the carefully-balanced tray without so much as the click of bronze on bronze. This was the Divine Daughter's bedchamber, and although it was empty, it was resonant with the holiness of a temple. The air smelled of her perfume. He was as careful as he always was, but he still felt an impetus to hurry. He would take the lamps from the Divine Daughter's private apartments down to the oil-store in the cellar to clean and refill them, and once that task was done, he would be able to do those of the infants' rooms. It was his favourite part of the day. Few were trusted with the daily tasks of their mistress' apartments, and fewer still were permitted near her children.

The prince and the princesses, the children of the Divine Daughter, would be a month old on the following day. They had been born small, but strong, and now they throve and grew. Three babies at one birth, and all survived — not one of the women in the palace had ever heard of such a thing. Skarritha's mercy was boundless. He-Redeems loved them as passionately as he did Barley's unborn baby, perhaps even more. He could almost regret that Barley's pregnancy had not occurred at the same time as that of his mistress. She might then have been chosen as a wetnurse for one of the babies. If the god meant her child to die anyhow, at least that would have given her something greater to love.

So far, Barley's condition remained a secret between the three of them, but despite this Barley cried at night when she got to brooding on what might come. Like First-Son, she was unable to trust to Skarritha's infinite wisdom. He-Redeems wished Barley could be permitted to see the babies, the grandchildren of Almighty Skarritha. In their presence it was so easy to feel a calm, peaceful assurance that Korthan lay in the lap of the god, loved and secure from all dangers beyond. Small worries of individual lives and deaths shrank to their true size, then. All were under the sheltering hand of the god. If only Barley and First-Son could learn to understand that.

He-Redeems took the last lamp and went back into the receiving room, closing the door softly behind him.

"Sir —?" he began to ask, turning to see a man moving towards him. He thought for a moment the Hound was one of the small troop, the Hand, that were the Great Lady's personal bodyguard. But he was not. He-Redeems knew all nine of those men and women well. This man was a stranger, and the woman behind him also.

And then the feet were kicked out from beneath him and he fell, tray and lamps flying, remnants of oil spattering across the floor and wall. Slaves learnt not to fight back, ever. He yelped and curled up, arms wrapped around his head, as someone kicked him again, calling him ... *heretic?*

He did not understand that. He tried to pull himself into a smaller space, but they grabbed his arms and hauled him up, two Hounds, and were dragging him across the room before he had his feet under him.

"I didn't do it," he cried. "Sirs, please, I've done nothing. I didn't do it."

He had no idea what he might have done, but he was certain he had done nothing, nothing at all, in all his life, that the thonor would care about, nothing even that the chamberlain might discipline him for, beyond keeping Barley's secret.

"Please," he begged, trying to hang back and only hurting himself. "Please, oh please, what have I done? And you can't leave that mess in there, my mistress might slip in the oil, please ..." To his shame he was starting to cry.

"Stop whining," the woman Hound said. He-Redeems bit his lip, trying to bite down the panic with it. They had mistaken him for someone else, they must have, that they came for him this way, as if he could hurt them, as if he were an enemy. His heart was pounding so that he could barely hear anything, just a strange roaring, like he was drowning, and the floor moved under his feet like a river's flowing. He scrabbled for footing on the stairs, stairs ... they were very far away, not flat at all but sickening, unsteady. They came rushing up to meet him, hitting him, hard, and a Hound swore, his voice stretched out and distant.

He fainted, like a girl.

Sound came back first, his ears ringing, and then a burst of pain as someone slapped his face. He-Redeems tried to lie still, so they would go away, but he was slapped again, harder. His eyes opened by themselves, and he whimpered.

"Good enough," said the Hound, rising from where he knelt over He-Redeems' body. "You'll wait here, heretic, until the Great Lady is ready to deal with you."

"I'm not, sir, please, I'm not ..." But the words bubbled through blood from a split lip and both the thonor were leaving, closing a door, shutting out all light.

"I'm no heretic!" he wailed after them. "Please! Some-one's told you lies, sirs. Please! I swear, by holy Skarritha's name!"

But he was alone, and no-one answered. He flung him-self flat on his face and prayed, for Skarritha's mercy, for Skarritha's forgiveness for whatever unwitting sin, what-ever wicked thought, had earned him such punishment. But he was no heretic. Never that. He prayed, and he wept.

In time there were footsteps outside, and a woman's sobbing. The noise drew nearer, passed, and the woman shrieked. The footsteps faded away but the screaming and sobbing went on, wordless rage and terror. He shut it out, closed himself up in his prayers.

When there were no words left for praying, when all his being was simply a quiet devotion to the god again, He-Redeems sat in the farthest corner of the small room, his arms wrapped around his knees, and waited. There was no light except a thin line under the door. He did not mind. Skarritha was light and darkness both, day and night, and night in day. He had brought night to day, eclipsing the sun to proclaim the advent of his reign as a mortal woman in Korthan. He could bring light to this darkness, to He-Redeems' penitent heart. If he was to die, Skarritha, who knew and saw all, would know He-Redeems was no heretic, no matter what the priests or the judges or the thonor believed. Skarritha knew his soul was pure.

The woman sobbed more quietly now, the sound worn hoarse and weak.

"Don't be afraid," he called. "Skarritha knows the innocent."

There was silence, and then a voice barely recognizable as Barley's called, "He-Redeems? He-Redeems! They're going to kill us as h-h-heretics." She stuttered on the word, barely able to get it out, and burst into tears again. For the first time he got up and tried the door. It was locked.

"Don't be afraid," he said again. "I know you're a true worshipper of Skarritha. Everyone knows. It'll be all right."

"They're going to kill us," she said dully, when her tears at last gave out. "They're going to take us to the temple and cut our throats. Or burn us." She didn't seem able to stop sobbing, but now it was a dry, gulping noise, nothing more.

"Everyone knows we're not."

"No-one will speak for us, He-Redeems. Don't be a f-f-fool. They'd be as good as accusing themselves too. Even First-Son won't dare." She drew a long, sighing breath. "I wish they'd locked us up together."

"So do I."

It would be a comfort, to be with Barley. But they shouldn't need such comfort. Skarritha held them in his hand, always. The god knew his own. He said as much to Barley, and she agreed, faintly, that yes, Skarritha knew his own.

The light under the door faded away. No-one came with water or food.

"He-Redeems?"

"What, Barley?"

"Pray for me? I'm not a very good person. We don't have time to pray, in the kitchens. And I get angry, when I think they'll take my baby away. I think it isn't fair the god made me be born a slave, and I know I should accept what's sent, that we're all Skarritha's but ... but sometimes I wonder if we aren't. I never meant to be bad. I thought maybe things would be different if — if they — if it was true they would come back .... And now I'll never have the baby at all. Pray for me, for mercy."

He had no idea what she was talking about, but it didn't matter. She was too distraught to make sense. "Don't cry," he said. Her voice was nothing now but a hoarse croak, and his little better. "Don't. Of course I'll pray for you. I always do."

"You're always so good. It's so easy for you. But I want to be with Skarritha when I die. I do. I do! Skarritha forgive me! I don't want to be damned, I don't want to be alone in the darkness."

"You won't be. Skarritha knows you're innocent. Go to sleep now, Barley. I'll pray."

And he did, shaping the words in his head, with soundless, painful lips, until he drifted into sleep himself.

he-Redeems slept badly, waking often to an empty stomach and a parched and painful throat. He dreamed of drinking, of jars of cool water and of the river, wide and slow. And in his dreams he could not get the water to his mouth; it ran from his hands, or he floated away as he reached for it. What woke him for good was Barley's crying out again, desperate, "He-Redeems! He-Redeems!"

There was daylight under the door once more. He flung himself down, saw sandals and thick male ankles on either side of slim bare feet that stumbled and staggered in passing by, and then they were gone, up the unseen stairs, and she was still calling his name. And then she wailed, "First-Son!" and he heard nothing more except another door closing.

The day passed. Water became the entirety of his thoughts. This was beyond thirst, a driving madness. He ceased to worry even about Barley, ceased almost from prayerful thoughts, except the drumming litany of *Skarritha, water* — plea or command or curse He-Redeems could not have said.

When they finally came for him he was lying curled up, mindless and unresponsive as a wounded animal. The Hounds dragged him up the stairs into the courtyard; it wasn't until the noon sun struck him in the eyes that He-Redeems groaned and began to struggle upright.

They let him stand, holding him, and waited while he blinked his sight back.

The first thing he saw was a body hanging from the gallery. It swayed and turned gently in the breeze.

The man had not been hanged. The corpse was black with caked and stinking blood from the chest on down, a wound back and front, with broken, jagged rib-bone showing. It shimmered, seethed, with a skin of flies.

It was First-Son. His eyes were gone, and a crow circled over the yard, cawing.

"Friend of yours?" said a Hound.

He-Redeems choked, felt the world going distant again. He dug nails into his own palms and dropped his head, eyes shut. A Hound jerked it up again, and he wrenched himself loose, his throat, his whole body heaving, fell to his knees and was sick, little though there was in his belly.

"Now that's a proper reverence for the apostate," one of the thonor said, and they dragged him up again, to lead him along under the gallery.

They were heading for the reception rooms, where the Great Lady entertained her guests. He was filthy, unwashed, he couldn't come before her so, and for a moment that was all he could think of, the insult his presence must offer her.

He could not believe, as soon as it was out of his sight, that that thing back there had been First-Son. It could not be. It must not.

Tears leaked from his eyes, ran down his face, stinging the rawness of his lips. At least Barley had not been hanging there too.

They took him into the White Room, the walls of which were of unrelieved white plaster, the floor of white-glazed brick. It was a very big, empty room, rarely used except when a governor or priest was called before the Great Lady for a reprimand. A black-lacquered chair sat against the far wall.

They shoved him down to the floor and stepped away. He-Redeems huddled with his face to the floor, praying. He could form no words of his own, whispered instead the invocation the priests used every morning, a great presumption. He was not worthy to utter the words.

He fell silent when he heard the rustling of stiff skirts across the floor, the tapping of sandals, the heavier tread of armoured soldiers.

"Did you see what is hanging in the courtyard?" the Divine Daughter's voice asked.

"The Great Lady speaks to you. Look up," a Hound said, and jabbed him with naked sword, hard enough to leave blood welling on his arm.

He-Redeems raised his head, shaped the word, yes, but could give it no breath. It seemed to be enough for her.

"A slave of my house," she said. "My house, born in my house, and he went out by secret ways to meet with apostates and heretics. Do you know what they did, He-Redeems-His-Father?"

It was the first time she had used his name since asking it, years before.

"Mistress," he croaked. "I know nothing."

"They met, every first quarter of the moon, to pray to gods whose names they did not know, gods who are long gone from Korthan. They told one another that there would be no sickness, no sorrow in all Korthan, if only they could have the old gods back, the gods who set all the cities of the plain to fighting, who sat by and let kings and dark sorcerers oppress their worshippers. The heretics whispered and plotted to find sorcerers, to bring them to the city, to overthrow our rule, they hoped. We are fortunate indeed they found none."

"Yes, mistress."

"Do you know what they were, He-Redeems-His-Father?"

"Mistress," he protested. "I know nothing of them."

"They were greedy, foolish men who dreamed of setting themselves over their fellows, who felt Skarritha had not rewarded them as was their due. They did not want to accept what Skarritha in his infinite wisdom decreed for them. So like sulky children running to grandmother, they made a little game of heresy, trying to lure the Nine back. But First-Son, this slave of my household — what do you know of him, He-Redeems-His-Father?"

He-Redeems only shook his head.

"You were very close. Unnaturally close, some would say. Did you never go with him down into the city?"

"Mistress, I never go to the city, except to the temple on the holy days, when I'm permitted."

She was not so much listening to his words, he felt, as tasting or smelling them, following like a hound back into his soul, to find what was truly there.

"Did he never show you what he had found while repairing the shelves, the broken passage at the back of the oil-cellar, that led into the sewer and the canal?"

"No, mistress."

"You are known to be a very devout man, He-Redeems-His-Father. Did he never suggest to you that your piety was misplaced?"

"No, mistress."

She waited. She knew.

"He mocked me, Great Lady," He-Redeems whispered weakly. "But it was only teasing, mistress. He called me 'priest's-boy'. That was all. Because I had served in the temple. He ... he felt I prayed too much. Maybe ... maybe he felt I presumed to a priest's sanctity, that I should be humbled. I never meant any offence to the god."

"No. Do you defend him?"

"I ... mistress, Great Lady, he was my friend." His heart hammered wildly. "He ... I knew nothing of any evil in him. If... if you say it is true, Great Lady ..."

"*If?*" she asked.

"... then I must believe you. Mistress ..." and he looked at her, pleading, meeting her eyes without flinching, as he never had when he shared her couch. "Please, mistress. Is it true?"

"Yes," she said.

He bowed his face back to the floor.

"Such heretics cannot expect to exist in Korthan unnoticed," she said, very gently. "Thonor found their meeting place, learned their names. First-Son was recognized and followed home a month ago. The night before last he was taken at their meeting, He-Redeems, and killed as he sought to flee. A coward's death."

Skarritha forgive him, he had seen First-Son coming back from that meeting a month before, mud on his feet, coming across the yard, yes, from the cellar where the oil-store was. He had seen an armed man following him, too, and had said nothing. Skarritha forgive him.

First-Son, forgive him.

"Imagine, He-Redeems. First-Son thought he would offer prayers to the damned and outcast Nine, and he had no names to call them by. Do you think his gods heard him?"

She did want an answer to that, stared as though her eyes could see the thoughts forming before they ever rode his tongue. And the thought that formed first of all was that she herself had lain with a son of the Nine, that yellow-eyed young man, the monster who had got her with child and escaped, and was not that worse than praying to gods whom everyone knew Skarritha had long ago defeated?

"In the temple they say the Nine answer prayers only to deceive, mistress, if they ever do at all."

"But what do you think?"

"Mistress?"

She waited.

"I never think about the Nine at all, Great Lady, except to pray that merciful Skarritha will keep all your cities safe from their evil."

"Do you pity your friend, He-Redeems? Do you mourn him?"

"I ..." But he could not, must not, lie to Skarritha's Daughter. He looked up again, somewhere about the belt of her gown, which was cloth of gold, the gown she wore to the temple rituals. Rituals ... if any of the heretics had survived their capture, they would have been executed in the temple, to purify Korthan again. "Mistress, he was my friend. I grieve that my friend was so deceived and fell into such evil ways. I ... I would wish him alive, Great Lady, and a good, god-fearing man, as I know he used to be, before he went astray. If he were alive I would pray that great Skarritha lead him back to right belief. But it is too late for that, and he is damned. So I must not pity him. I hate his sin."

"Yet you loved him."

"I could not love a heretic, mistress."

"You shared the kitchen-girl Barley with him."

"Mistress, please. Barley knows no more than me about First-Son. He loved her. He would never have risked damning her soul."

"But he might have deceived himself and believed he saved it."

"He would never have risked her, mistress. No matter what sin he committed himself."

"He talked to her of the Nine. He taught her prayers. He would have taught them to the child she carried. Your child, He-Redeems-His-Father."

"My ... mine? Mistress, I know it was wrong of us to keep it secret. Please, please forgive us that, her and me. But you are a mother, you know how she must feel, and I know no matter how she listened to First-Son, she never believed anything wicked, she was just foolish, mistress, she said, just this morning, last night, she prayed for Skarritha's mercy ..."

A Hound struck him, with the flat of the heavy bronze blade this time, and he went cold and hot and nearly threw up again.

"Forgive me, mistress," he whispered again, shaking where he crouched, eyes once more fixed on the floor. But he could not seem to keep silent. "Forgive her. She was only foolish. You must know that, in your mercy. She surely only thought it a game. She repents now, I know she does."

His teeth clattered together with his shivering.

"Your son, not the heretic's," the Divine Daughter said. "But what if he had claimed it his, raised it his in the pattern of his evil, corrupted it as he corrupted the girl? Would you have shut your eyes to it, remained ignorant of sin, then? Would she have whispered prayers of the lying Nine over it, and would you have let her?"

"Mistress, I knew nothing."

"Yes. I know. A man less innocent and godly would have suspected more. Tell me, He-Redeems-His-Father, what I should do with you."

"Mistress?"

"What am I to do with you? You are a good man. You are a loyal and devout man. I see it in you. I see your innocence. You were deceived, gravely deceived. You will examine the souls of your friends and bedmates more closely in future and not assume that all people are as virtuous as yourself. But I cannot have in my household a slave who has been tainted, however innocently, with apostasy. So what shall I do with you?"

"You are merciful," he whispered. "Send me back to the temple, mistress. I shall pray every hour to be worthy of your forgiveness and great Skarritha's."

She looked at him, looked *through* him, sifting every sinful thought, every grumble, every failure. He huddled smaller, ashamed, wishing she would order him killed, set him on a quick, clean path to union with Skarritha.

"Perhaps, in time," she said, slowly, "perhaps, you will be worthy to serve in my palace again. I remember you have always been faithful, devoted, always been true in your heart. But you must be punished, for the well-being of the slaves' halls. They must see justice."

"You are merciful, mistress. I'm not worthy."

"But you may be again. You will be banished to one of the estates, He-Redeems-His-Father, or — no. The-Cow-Eyed, your Hand has done well in this. I give this man to you, for the time being. You are not to kill him or sell him; I may ask for his return some day."

"Thank you, mistress," a woman said from somewhere behind him.

"And that is that," the Divine Daughter muttered. "Captain, your Hand has three days' leave."

The woman's voice murmured acceptance of that, and the Great Lady's footsteps left, followed by others. He-Redeems looked up for a last glimpse of her, something to carry in his heart until he was fit to return to her nearer service. He saw only the back of her heavy gown, a cascade of black hair, and two of her own Hand of thonor, bright in armour of bronze scales, walking close on her heels. The door shut between them.

"Up," one of the remaining Hounds said, nudging him with a foot, and He-Redeems stood, swaying, eyeing his new masters.

The Hound's mouth twisted. "He stinks."

"So wash him." That was a third Hound, the woman by the outer door. Half her face was black, bruised, and her lip was torn, probably as painful as He-Redeems' own. "Leave, boys. Take him to the barracks and let's find a tavern."

They left, shoving He-Redeems along with them. Thonor didn't march. They strode in a ragged pack, seeming connected as if by invisible ropes, always aware of the precise location of their fellows, always alert, to react on the drawing of a breath.

The Divine Daughter had a company of thonor garrisoned in the palace itself, and others in barracks on the plaza and in the city. He was relieved to see they were going through the palace, not out onto the plaza. This Hand was of the palace company. He would not be leaving the palace, not leaving the Great Lady's vicinity.

They went through a series of ground-floor rooms, through a heavy door, and then they were out in a courtyard he had not known existed. The barracks was like a separate building, with its own courtyard, its own gallery and well. The air smelt of the kitchens, of pork and onions. His throat spasmed and he clenched his teeth, to stop his stomach heaving again.

"Wash-room and laundry," the Hand-captain said, pointing in under the gallery. "Clean yourself. Slaves' hall is by the kitchens. My Hand's hall's up off the gallery, there. Find Tamarind. He's ours, too."

She pointed, slapped his shoulder, not unkindly, and ran up the nearest gallery stairs, the other two following.

He-Redeems stood where they had left him.

The grunts and shouts and laughter of the Hounds exercising in the courtyard were very far away, floating on a sort of beelike buzzing. And the sun was very hot, the air sticky with the last of the rainy season humidity. He felt a little as if he were floating in a dream, as if it would all fade away and he would wake, holding tightly to First-Son and Barley, holding them so they would never slip from him again.

Instead, he walked in the direction the Hand-captain had indicated, and found the wash-room, a long room with a bitumen-sealed floor and a drain, brick benches around the walls, a few copper cauldrons and a row of empty jars. Two slaves, a man and an older woman, were laundering clothes and swapping gossip about their Hands. They fell silent, eyeing He-Redeems suspiciously. He ignored them and they said nothing, went back to their tasks in silence.

Water. He trudged, staggering crookedly, to the well, and pulled down the long beam to raise the pail. His hands shook as he filled the jar, but he made it all the way back to the wash-room before he plunged his face in, sucking the water like a greedy animal. He stopped when his belly began to cramp, stripped, with slow and clumsy fingers, and began dipping water over himself. Then he drank some more, poured water over his gown and wrung it out, and just sat, shivering, his back against the bench.

He was supposed to find someone, but the name had slipped away from him. Everything had. The two doing laundry had left, and the wash-room was quiet, peaceful.

"Wake up, palace boy."

A bare foot was planted in front of his face. He-Redeems sat up slowly. He had tipped over where he huddled, stark naked, on the wash-room floor.

He peered up at a middle-aged man, broad-faced and grey around the temples. In the palace, they called the slaves who served in the barracks kitchens and the slaves belonging to the thonor "Hound's meat," or worse, but that automatic response to "palace boy" died barely thought.

"You the heretic, palace boy?"

"'m not," he muttered, groping for his clothes, which were still sopping.

"Yeah, so they said. Innocent of Nine-worshipping, but not too bright. I'm Tamarind."

"He-Redeems-His-Father." He-Redeems got his gown over his head, stood, swaying, to pull on his drawers. He fell, but the bench was under him then.

"They beat you?" Tamarind asked, with detached interest.

He-Redeems shook his head. A few kicks were not a beating.

"You look half-dead. Turtle said you fainted a couple times. You prone to that?"

Another silent denial. "I just ... I haven't had anything to eat since breakfast. Yesterday. Or to drink." He waved a hand at the empty jar. "Till now. I'm not sick. Really."

Tamarind might be happy to have a fellow to share his work; he wouldn't be if he thought he was going to end up responsible for a weakling.

"Ah. Well, come on then. It'd better be the kitchens."

He-Redeems staggered gratefully after him.

"So," said Tamarind, as they walked along under the gallery. "I heard, well, you're innocent of heresy and all that, right, but still, the kind of people you called your friends ... I heard they didn't kill you only because, um ... the Great Lady... were you ...? I mean, did you, you know — with *her*? The Divine Daughter herself?"

"It was a long time ago," he said dully.

Tamarind pursed up his lips. "Hah. Well." He gave He-Redeems a lingering, sidelong look.

In the cavernous kitchen there was bread and a bowl of boiled lentils, and a number of curious glances and whisperings. He-Redeems didn't see Barley anywhere, and realized he had been expecting to. If he was sent away, so would she be, and maybe to the barracks kitchen.

"What about the kitchen-girl?" he asked Tamarind quietly.

"Kitchen-girls? Lots of kitchen-girls, take your pick."

"Barley. She was locked up. But she was innocent too. She prayed to Skarritha. The Great Lady can see our hearts. She knows Barley loves Skarritha, truly. She'll show mercy. Did they send Barley here too?"

"No."

"Oh." He cleaned out the bowl with the last piece of bread, handed it back to the old woman who had brought it. "They must have sent her off to the country, then."

Poor Barley. She'd never been out of the palace in her life. He didn't even think she had ever been beyond the gates onto the plaza. A country estate would be a foreign land, to her.

And he would never see her again.

"Ah, that kitchen-girl," Tamarind said.

"You must have heard."

"Um, yes. Forget her. She's gone. Come on back to our hall, you can sleep or something. Not much to do right now, actually. They're all off in the city and I've done all the chores."

"You go," He-Redeems said. "I want to look around. If that's all right?"

"I suppose. Stay out of people's way, don't get yourself beaten up, captain won't like it."

"Yes. Thanks."

He followed Tamarind back out to the courtyard, watched to see which gallery door he entered. They didn't want him thinking about Barley, of course they didn't, didn't want him doing anything that would make people think about heresy. The poison of the Nine was contagious. He should thank Skarritha Tamarind was charitable enough not to treat him like he had some sort of catching plague.

But Barley wouldn't know what had happened to him. She might be thinking of him like ... the other one ... dead and bloating in the sun as an example to the rest. If he could learn where Barley had been sent, he might be able to get word to her, so that she would know he was alive, and forgiven, as she was surely forgiven. But she would need comfort.

And the baby would be a boy, a son for them — for the two of them. He would grow in the Daughter's service on whatever estate Barley was at, he would be loved, he would serve the Great Lady ... maybe someday He-Redeems would even be able to see him.

He walked through the heavy door separating the barracks from the palace, walked the old familiar rooms and narrow passageways feeling already a stranger, an intruder, avoiding the central yard where First-Son's body would be hanging. He could hear crows, squawking and squabbling. He clenched his teeth, refusing to think of it, and headed down the wide stairs to the palace kitchens. A butcher flattened himself against the wall as He-Redeems passed, holding his basket high, and muttered, "Skarritha bless," as though he were a ghost.

He-Redeems couldn't catch anyone's eye. People he had known looked away, found errands that took them up the other stairs. A girl who had been Barley's closest friend among the women turned her back when he spoke.

He still felt weak, sick, *tired*, from going so long without water or food. He felt like lying down where he was, weeping like a baby. "I just want someone to tell Barley ..." he started to shout at them all, when an old woman plucked at his sleeve.

"Shut up," she said. "Come along. This is no place for you. We can't have your kind in here, getting us all in trouble. Barley wouldn't want that."

The last words silenced him and he followed docilely, towed towards the stairs. But then she jerked him in behind one of the brick counters.

"Sit," she ordered, hissing toothlessly, and he sat on the debris-covered floor. The old woman thumped the pot of honey she carried down on the counter, took up a pestle and began pounding a big mortar full of nuts.

"I've seen you around. Nice boy, I always thought, if a bit dim. Good boy for my Barley. Thought that about the other one too. Ugly boy, but kind. And smart."

"You're Barley's mother?"

"Grandmother. Poor child. I thought the Hounds had you."

"No." He swallowed. "I mean, yes. I'm to serve Hand-Captain The-Cow-Eyed now."

"The mistress looks after her favourites, I see." She sniffed, poured a dollop of honey into the nuts, catching a drop on her crooked finger and licking it. "Don't come here again. Don't ask about Barley. You'll get others in trouble, and they won't escape."

"But Barley. Is she sent to the country? I thought someone could take word to her, so she wouldn't worry. Is she still here?"

His voice was rising. The old woman hissed at him.

"She loved First-Son. Loved the both of you. Were you truly his friend, or you just put up with him to have Barley? Or, hah, you put up with her to have him?"

"No!" he protested. "I loved them both. Skarritha forgive me," he added, angry, afraid.

"And you a good, pious boy. Your friend had some secret way out of the palace into the city, they say. They say he met with Nine-worshippers and they lay with goats and drank the blood of newborn boys to call up the outcast gods." She snorted. "More fools them that say it. They'll know better one day, and soon. But the Great Lady spared you, for your pretty eyes, I suppose."

"Because I was innocent. I never knew where First-Son went, or what he did."

And he would never have done anything like she said, goats and babies, not First-Son. That was ... nonsense. If First-Son was apostate, then it was because ... because he believed something. First-Son always wanted something *better*.

Better than the god.

"Innocent! That you are. Not like poor young Barley, who couldn't even say who fathered her child. No, the Daughter wouldn't throw such innocence as yours away. She needs that. Tastes it like honey, I suppose. Not much of it around. Innocence and pretty eyes, and her bed's empty again, isn't it?"

As though the Daughter were any foolish girl from the weaving hall.

"The Great Lady did no wrong," he said stiffly.

"Oh no. Not to you and the others, my innocent boy, picked up and tossed aside like toys, eh? Not to First-Son stinking up the courtyard. Or my poor Barley. Never. All her acts are holy, our great mistress. Skarritha *bless* her. Such innocence. Such devotion! Only the gods deserve such, boy." And all the time she was grinding and thumping with the pestle, dropping more nuts in, more honey. But she looked up then, a flash of dark eyes, and down at her paste again.

"But where's Barley?" He-Redeems demanded.

"Beyond your saving, poor child."

Stupidly, he asked, "What do you mean?"

"Dead."

"But why? Barley wasn't ..." He whispered it. "She wasn't a heretic. She never believed what First-Son said. She just did it to please First-Son. She wasn't heretic. Was she?"

"It would be all right if she were, then? Like your beloved friend First-Son out there? That's all right?"

He-Redeems shook his head.

"Maybe she believed and maybe she didn't. She was screaming for Skarritha's mercy when they took her away. Doesn't matter, does it? She was contaminated, defiled. She slept with him. You see?"

"But ..." So had he.

"Barley didn't have your face to save her," the old woman said. "Hah. And then again, maybe she did, they both had you and that didn't help matters, eh? The Great Lady's a woman in the end, after all. Jealous of her toys even after she tires of them."

"Where is she?" he whispered, barely hearing. "Barley, where is she? Not ... out there? Did they... did they take her to the temple?"

"No. No to both. Those prisoners that survived the Hounds were all burnt this morning in the yard of the public temple, 'cept two the Great Lady killed on the altar. To testify to the glory of Skarritha, you know. I had permission. Went down to see."

He-Redeems was revolted. "Why?"

"Why? Why witness such a holy act, the cleansing of the city of such evil? A good pious boy like you has to ask?

Why did I go? To say a few prayers for their souls. But
your Barley ..." She reached out and took both his hands.
"I'm sorry, He-Redeems. The priests took her out for the
adulteress's death."

An adulteress taken in the act could be sewn into a sack
weighted with rocks, and thrown into the river.

"She ... *Barley*?"

"They took her right away from judging in the White
Room this morning, Hounds and priests and the chamberlain. Down to the river. It was a betrayal of the household,
they say the mistress decreed, like an adulterous wife's betrayal, and so that end for her."

"Barley's *dead*?"

The old woman's grip on his hands tightened. "You do
your weeping in private, boy, as I do. The Daughter can
still change her mind about your so-innocent and devoted
soul."

"But Barley ..."

"It's a better death than burning, I imagine. I tell myself. I pray. Now, get out of here, and don't come back."

He-Redeems got slowly to his feet, moving like an old
man, and turned away.

"And I will pray for your eyes to be opened," she muttered behind him. "Because First-Son thought you were
worth loving. Poor fool. And so did my sweet Barley."

He took the wrong stairs, climbed to the courtyard and
stood dully beneath the pillars, looking across the yard. Not
even a man, from here, not First-Son. Just a shape, and the
crows ripping at it. And the flies seething. Never First-Son.

He bit his lip and swallowed hard, blinking, but the
tears came anyway. Wrong to weep for ... that. He forced
his mind to holiness, to the greatest peace he knew, the
Daughter's three holy babies in their cradles, asleep, serene
... divine, the presence of the god in the world.

If his unborn child was evil because of Barley, who only listened, surely only listened, who called on Skarritha at the end, if the child was not saved for He-Redeems' innocence or its own, for his devoted worship ... could even the Daughter's virtue redeem her babies, fathered not by mere heresy but by the very blood of the Nine?

So those babies you think so beautiful and holy are evil and outcast far more than Barley's would have been. Or if they're innocent babies, yours must be innocent too. Which is it? First-Son's thoughts in his mind; he would never think such things on his own, never.

First-Son was dead, and they would never lie close together in the slaves' hall again, whispering. He swallowed again against the choking in his throat. Heretic. Cast him out of his mind.

There's no justice in Skarritha. No mercy, if even a baby can't be forgiven. First-Son's thoughts. But they weren't. They were He-Redeems' own, and he could not pretend otherwise.

He felt in memory an arm over him, warm, hard-muscled body close. Whispering breath on his ear. *Priest's boy. So that's great Skarritha's mercy? Tell Barley it's justice, then. Look me in the eyes and tell me it was justice for Barley. Tell our son. Your son.* He gagged at the smell and staggered on his way to the barracks, walking near without looking up, to see what was not left of the face.

He-Redeems sat in his hand's hall, hemming a new gown. It was easy work, mindless. *Merciful Skarritha, merciful Skarritha, merciful Skarritha ...* the words grew empty in his mind. The evening sun shone in through the open door, staining the far wall red.

The Hand wouldn't be coming back from the tavern that evening, his fellow slave told him, and maybe not till morning. Hounds did not have to worry about the city curfew.

Tamarind brought food up for their evening meal. "Spare you facing the slaves' hall till tomorrow," he said.

He-Redeems knew he ought to thank the man, couldn't make himself speak, and didn't touch the food.

"A quick death, anyway," Tamarind said then, and he knew he had been watched, leaving the barracks. Tamarind had known why he was going. "Better than burning."

"Yes."

Quick? Less pain, maybe. He prayed so.

Who to? Skarritha who ordered it, with the voice of his Divine Daughter?

Go away, he told his own thoughts. And imagined that First-Son smiled, angry, taunting. *Priest's boy.*

Eventually Tamarind ordered him to bed, closing the door but leaving a lamp burning in a niche in case their masters should return. He-Redeems lay stiffly at the edge of the mat, listening to Tamarind breathing. He was too aware of the man, a presence too close, too ... not First-Son. It was too quiet, not the great crowd breathing and muttering, the slow breaths and fast, the lonely whimpers and the furtive joinings of the slaves' hall. He wanted to weep, now, and could not, not with Tamarind there to hear. He could not jerk his mind away from Barley. Barley warm and sharp-boned, pressed against him, turning from him to First-Son and back again, the three of them one tangled urgent knot. Barley struggling to breathe in the dark water, fighting the heavy cloth. Barley gasping and nothing but water entering her lungs, burning, and the weight of the water over her and stones, pulling her down ....

But some time in the night he remembered, *Such innocence. Such devotion. Only the gods deserve such, boy,* and he thought, *the gods?* Not something First-Son had ever said, and not that voice of his own in his head that he lied in calling First-Son, either. His mind jerked away from Barley.

The old woman in the kitchens talked of the gods? He had spoken with an apostate in the Divine Daughter's own kitchen.

The Great Lady must be warned.

The voice he was calling First-Son laughed at him.

He felt water burning in his lungs, saw the old woman's dark eyes, sharp and knowing as youth, Barley's eyes. The old kitchen-woman was not some dodderer betrayed by a wandering mind. She gave him those words.

First-Son thought you were worth loving. And so did my sweet Barley.

He rolled over, staring towards the dim lamp. His heart felt swollen, closing off his throat, an ache he could not swallow. But his eyes were dry, all weeping burned away.

It had been all he thought he needed, Skarritha's love. And First-Son and Barley, the baby, only pieces of it, lamp-lights to the god's great sun of love.

The lamps remained real, hot in his heart. The other was ... a distant mirror, only reflecting, not burning.

They were gone, and the world was empty, and he would not be with them, ever. All the family he ever had, all the love he had ever given and received. He would never be with them, not even in the great union with Skarritha to come in the end of days, since the god granted them no mercy, rejected them, condemned by the Divine Daughter's word.

Did the outcast Nine take in Skarritha's outcasts? Was that son of an outcast goddess who still eluded all the hunting thonor, that golden-eyed monster for whom the Great Lady had turned him from her bed, that unholy father of the three holy babies, a sign of the Nine's return to Korthan?

Tamarind rested an arm over him, a body warm and close against his back. An attempt at comfort, maybe; maybe, from the looks the man had given him, the closest to the Divine Daughter he would ever come. He-Redeems did not bother to edge away as the man pressed nearer. It did not seem to matter.

Great Nine gods, he tried, shaping words with no breath, as First-Son had always prayed. *Great Nine. Are you there?*

the inexorable tide

I am an old woman now, and my granddaughter's children play at battles through my orchard, but I hear other voices in the murmur of the leaves, in the hum of the bees and the whisper of the waves along the shore. I see other forms, so beloved, so familiar, in the mists of the lake that hides our last refuge. I remember.

If Livy and Plutarch teach us anything, it is that time is relentless. It presses on, heavy with the weight of peoples, with Fate and Fortune, and in the end it rolls over us, swamps even the best.

We were far from the best. I was not my father; Amhar had no chance to be his; Mordred was ... simply Mordred. Though valiant in battle, he was not the fiery hero his brother Gawain was, and he was not his uncle; he could have been an Arthur in a different style, a builder and restorer, if Arthur had given us a lasting peace.

It seemed at the time as though he had. The Saxon heathen were driven from Britain, the warring kings and dukes swept into Arthur's orbit. Merlin was gone, sleeping in his cave, or so the songs already said, and I, his daughter, said nothing to deny it. Now the songs say other things of me, of all of us, and I smile and say nothing.

But Merlin was gone, and the Ladies on their island sent me to the King in his place, which a mere girl could not fill, not in that council of warriors. Arthur listened to me with the respect due my father and my training, but my words lacked the force of my father's prophecy, the strength of his vision.

The King was restless. He was not a lord for peace, though peace was ever his driving dream. When Hoel in Brittany begged aid against the heretic Visigoths on his borders, Arthur's answer was shaped as much by desire to be doing as by kinship's right.

Britain armed. The old heroes, Bedwyr and Cai, Gawain and even Mordred, felt their blood wake again. The young who dreamed of heroism, finding no beauty in the quiet farmstead, the green valley and the cattle grazing, could not be held back. The maids talked of champions, and sighed. Only the old mothers sat by the fire with shadows in their eyes, remembering what could be lost.

And I, I, Nimiane, went to the King.

He was a big man, and Roman-dark. In his presence lesser men dwindled, like candles held against the hearth. I found him with Bedwyr, as was usually the case.

"Cousin," I said, once we had exchanged the usual courtesies — "cousin" was always the style between us, as it had been between Arthur and my father. "Are you set on going to war for Hoel?"

"Hoel has always been a true friend to Britain," Arthur said, by which he meant, to himself as well. "He gave me aid when I most needed it. You would not counsel me to turn my back on him now?"

"No," I said. "I would never advise you to turn your back on your kinsman. But neither should you turn your back on Britain. Send a host to Hoel, by all means, but remain at home yourself."

"You'll make me old before my time," he said, laughing.

"As my father grew old before his, helping you to carry the burden of a kingdom, and suffering the spite of your enemies," I returned. "Your sword is needed here, cousin."

"Britain is at peace. The Saxons fear our very name."

"They fear your name. Lord, I beg you, send a host to Hoel, send Gawain and Mordred to show him honour, but don't go to Less Britain yourself."

"What do you fear, Nimiane?" Bedwyr asked.

"The King's enemies," I said. "Britain's enemies. If you go to Less Britain and take the greater part of Britain's armies with you, who defends us here?"

"I'll not leave Britain undefended," Arthur said.

"No? Does Bedwyr go with you?"

"Yes," Bedwyr answered.

"And Cai?"

Bedwyr snorted, and Arthur said, "Try to leave him behind."

"Gawain?"

"Of course. Mordred will stay," said the King. "That should please you, little cousin." He grinned, and I flushed. "Mordred and Guenevere will rule in my name," Arthur went on. "And you will remain, Nimiane, to advise them as your father advised me. In what better hands could I leave my kingdom?"

"Guenevere ..." I said. But what could I say of Guenevere, to her lord? What would my father have said? That she was growing old, and bitter, time slipping through her fingers? Her youth had faded in uncertainty and war, in waiting, without even a baby for comfort, to see Arthur carried home on a bier. Now she played games of courtship with the young warriors to fill her empty days, while Arthur's bastard Amhar admiringly trailed the heroes of the Saxon wars. Would Merlin have cautioned that power given as a sop now was either insult, or worse, excess, as wine after abstinence? I said nothing. I was not my father, to speak so to my King.

the ships carried the warriors of Britain away.

We were not left undefended, but those remaining behind were not the best, and they were not the greater part of the warbands. They were youths like Amhar, untried in war, or the old who had lost their taste for glory — who had learned sense, some might say.

All was well enough at first. From Brittany we heard report of battles and victories. Several more shiploads of warriors made the crossing, without Mordred's leave but with Guenevere's blessing. Her champions, she called them, sent to the King's banner, where she would be herself if she could. That led to bitter words in the hall.

"You must be reconciled," I told Mordred, after the worst of these exchanges with the Queen. "And now, before any rumour of quarrelling spreads."

Mordred sat slouched in a chair by my fire, legs stretched to the hearth, his cup of wine barely tasted on the table between us. He was fair as a Saxon changeling, with his uncle's black Roman eyes. He looked to me like a brooding angel, but I never claimed to be free of girlish fancies. Amhar sprawled at his feet, a dark youth, beginning to near Arthur's height and breadth of shoulder. Both spent more time in my small house than in the King's, now that Guenevere ruled it.

"She tried to send Amhar with the last band," Mordred said. "She as good as called him coward, when he refused to go."

"My father told me to look after Nimiane," Amhar remarked to the fire. "I didn't tell *her* that. I smiled, and walked out. She wants me dead, but it isn't as if she has any sons for me to threaten."

"And here I thought you adored me for my own sake." I poked Amhar with a bare toe. He rolled over, grinning, and grabbed my ankle.

"And what if I do?"

"Don't be foolish. And don't provoke the Queen." I withdrew my foot beneath my skirt, more disconcerted than I wanted to admit at the touch of skin on skin.

"Lecture Mordred, not me, cousin." Amhar sat up, leaning his shoulder against my knee, his gaze fixed on Mordred. "The men are taking sides. And you know, *Every kingdom divided against itself is brought to desolation.*"

I shivered, and the fire seemed dark.

"We'll be brought to desolation for certain if the Queen sends many more troops to Arthur," Mordred grumbled. "There was a report of longships off Rutupiae last month. Guenevere laughs and says they won't dare land for fear of the King, and it's an old man's timidity to keep men home for such a remote threat."

"The wolves circle." I spoke without thought, and paused to consider what the words might mean. "The King's name is great, but the King is not here. They will try us. Tell the queen — I'll tell the Queen, no more men must leave."

"Mordred should tell her," said Amhar. "She'll take it better from him."

"She will not," said Mordred. "She did not. You were there, Amhar."

"She will, if you charm her. She likes to be charmed."

"I don't want to charm her," Mordred snapped. He shoved himself upright in the chair with such force that the table beside it rocked. "She's a vain, spoilt child turned to a petulant harridan."

"But she is beautiful, and clever in a shallow way, and she likes to be told she is as wise as she is beautiful. Put it to her that way. Apologize for your temper. Smile sweetly. Say you know she is anxious for the King's return, but that perhaps her love for the King makes her incautious of the kingdom. Say Arthur trusts her to do what is best, to put Britain's good before his own. Say the warriors are eager to join Arthur, and only her words will keep them home to defend us. Make it her power that keeps men home, and so lead her into doing what must be done."

"You're a dangerous child," I said, and Amhar sat away from me.

"I'm hardly a child," he said coldly. "Guenevere is simple. She won't take your advice, Nimiane, because you're another woman, younger, beautiful, respected by the King. She thinks you have what she wants. But she'll do whatever Mordred tells her, if he only has the sense to court her a little."

"What do I have that she wants?" I asked.

Amhar snorted, and Mordred flung the wine, cup and all, into the fire.

"Court the hungry bitch yourself, Amhar," he said. "Nimiane, good night."

he came back later that evening, once Amhar had gone, so close on the heels of his young cousin's going that I knew he had been watching for it.

The fire had settled to a mound of glowing coals, shaping visions in the night — men fighting, men dying, but I could not see who they might be. Mordred stood between me and the hearth, a shadow limned in fire, like a saint or an emperor.

"Tell me what to do, Nimiane," he said. "Do I play the Queen's games to stop her sending the men away? Am I worrying over nothing, to fear a Saxon landing?"

"No," I said, speaking from the fleeting shapes in the flames, thinking of wolves, circling the flock, edging in to try if the shepherd and his dogs were wakeful. "No. The Saxons will come again, and the Picts from the north. The Queen must send no more men to Brittany. Do what you must, to persuade her of that."

Mordred stood in silence.

"Very well," he said at last. "I will charm her."

"Flatter her."

"Oh," he said, "she needs no flattery." His voice was heavy, defeated.

My father did not teach me to understand men, not in that way, and so I did not see Mordred's distaste for the fear and self-distrust it was, did not understand that a man might despise and still desire. I did not realize, until too late, that my concern to keep my own heart secret kept me from recognizing the very thing it desired. I said nothing, and sent him to Guenevere.

All I saw were longships, and the yellow-haired heathen wading ashore, and the farmsteads burning.

GUENEVERE hATEÔ BEÔWYR, who held more of Arthur's love than she ever could, and she had almost as strong a jealousy of Cai and Gawain and Mordred. They all shared something with Arthur, a past, a fellowship, that she thought she could not. She had always played at winning the love of Arthur's dearest comrades as a way of claiming a part in the glory, and in later years, I think, of assuring herself she still had beauty and the power it gives the powerless over men. But I do not believe she ever intended to betray the King in fact, until in his absence Mordred began to play her courting games.

I understand Amhar's meaning now — the Queen thought she was winning Mordred from me as well as from Arthur. Perhaps she was. Perhaps for her, the possibility of a double triumph was too much to resist.

Mordred looked sometimes like a man trapped in a tormenting dream. I shut my eyes to it, telling myself there was nothing I could do, if Mordred chose to go so far in placating her. I prayed to the King's God and to those of my father that no-one else should suspect. At least there were no more quarrels in the hall over keeping men home.

It was as well, for that summer the Picts came. We rode north with the speed that had won Arthur his early victories, arriving unexpected, and thrust them back. That was Amhar's first battle, and mine, though my work was with the wounded afterward.

We returned to find a Saxon raiding party had ventured up the Thames, sacking an abbey and escaping unhindered.

Mordred raised levies to watch the coast, and for a time all was quiet. He resumed his custom of sitting in my house in the evenings, which seemed to irritate the ever-present Amhar as much as his absence had done. He looked older, weary, as if some vital spirit had drained from him. Guenevere, I think, had tired of her conquest, and he was left with the guilt; Guenevere was not the sort to carry her own guilt.

She had tired of rule as well, and we were left to make decisions for Britain's continued defence without her interference. There was a handsome young harper at the King's fort, come from Hibernia, from Munster. He made songs to the Queen's glory before he went his wandering way again, richer for a gold arm-ring the Queen herself had worn.

Another season of campaigning passed, and another, and another. The heathen raids grew more frequent. Our summers went by in rapid riding and battle, and the unceasing watch for the longships. Our land had been without its king for years, by that time, and still Arthur did not return from Hoel's kingdom. Men began to doubt he ever would.

Then word came that in what was almost the last battle of the war against the Visigothic heretics in Brittany, Bedwyr had been slain. His death shattered the King; I think it brought home to Arthur his own mortality as nothing else could have done, and the years of warring seemed suddenly bereft of meaning. He decided to make a pilgrimage, to go to Rome. Guenevere read his letter to Mordred and me. Amhar was there too, uninvited, and the newly-returned harper of Munster, sitting at the Queen's feet.

"Rome!" I said, when she had finished. "What need has he of penance and pilgrimage? Arthur's wars were just wars. He fought for Christian Britain."

Mordred looked at me with a flash of his old boyish smile, so like his uncle's. We did not discuss before Guenevere what faith the Ladies held, or to whom my father had prayed.

"He fought for Britain's safety, not his own glory," I amended. "It's not Rome condemns him, but his own sorrow for Bedwyr's death. He must come home."

"There comes a time when every man must examine his own soul," said Guenevere. "It's not for us to stand between him and his Creator."

I thought her sanctimonious and smug, and looked away from Mordred, to catch the venomous look the Munsterman darted at him.

He knew. She had told the infatuated singer something of Mordred and herself. And the man had been several years away singing his songs; they would spread, as songs did, and grow.

Arthur must laugh at such songs, if ever they reached the pilgrim's road to Rome.

I wrote a letter to the King, and Mordred wrote. We told him of the Pictish invasion and Saxon raids, reminded him he carried Britain's strongest arms away with him.

We received no answer, and the tale was carried on the wind over the kingdoms, that Arthur the High King of Britain had laid aside his sword, that Arthur of Britain went afoot to Rome in a monk's robe, that the heroes of his warband, those who survived, went with him carrying holy relics.

This much is true, that Arthur set out for Rome, lingering at every shrine and every lord's hall, and the men who had followed him to Brittany followed him south.

So the Saxons massed, not mere raiders but armies, with a king, Childriche, to lead them. They saw the fat pastures of Britain undefended, open again for settlement. And they came.

Maybe we could have taken some other way. Maybe we should have fought to the bitter end, lost all, and died heroes, if any remained to remember us and sing our songs. Maybe we were not the best to be defending Britain, in that time.

Maybe. Fate and Fortune stood against us. The weight of history was too great, the press of shifting peoples too urgent; even the mighty legions had felt it as they fell back on Rome, leaving such as we behind. We did not have the swords to stand against the hosts of our enemies. Our strength was with Arthur on the road to Rome.

Mordred was king in all but name; he held the kings and dukes together, and Guenevere, more a queen than I think she had ever been, stood at his side to remind them by whose authority the Prince of Lothian commanded. Amhar, too, Arthur's son though not his heir, gave weight to Mordred's command, as did I.

Three great battles we fought against Childriche that summer; one we lost and in two we had the victory, and we held the Saxons back from the west.

But that was all. We could do no more, and the eastern shore was lost to us again. We made a peace; we allowed Childriche the lands he held. It was that or lose the whole; they could send wave after wave against us, and we were few.

Some cried that Mordred betrayed Arthur, ceding lands his uncle's men had paid for in blood, not even a generation ago. I say that Arthur, however innocently, betrayed Mordred, charging him with the realm's defence and taking from him the men who should have defended it.

We heard no word from Rome.

I dreamt of churned and bloody fields, burning villages, and heard a song of Mordred's lust for his uncle's queen. I dreamed myself Mordred's wife, and Amhar's, and could not choose between them. Guenevere made no secret of her love for the Harper of Munster, but out of bed she was a queen, and the lines that creased her face about the eyes and mouth became her better than her rose-petal beauty ever had.

Mordred and Amhar patrolled the coast and the line we had set for the Saxons; the Queen and I ruled the fort and held the kings and dukes together in Mordred's absence.

Early one morning, as I stood idly watching my servant stirring our porridge, I saw in the flames three ships drawn up on shore, and the tide ebbing. They had come in on the flood, sent scouts stealthily ashore. Now horses plunged over the side, men rode over the shingle, swords glinting in the dawn. They crested the dunes, gathering speed, shouting. The ships were not longships; the Saxons did not fight on horseback. Their cry was *Arthur*, and *Traitor to the King*.

I cried Mordred's name to the flames. My servant spilled the porridge-pot and ran for the Queen, seeing death in my eyes.

The shore patrol was mounted to meet the charge before any recognized its leader, and by then it was too late. Gawain was in no mind to talk. He cut down the first men to ride against him and made straight for Mordred his brother, battle-mad. The rage that had served Arthur so well betrayed his champion at the end; Gawain did not pause and would not listen. In preserving his own life Mordred left Gawain for dead, then broke his surviving men away. They rode for our stronghold while the attackers retreated to a nearby abbey, carrying their dying leader.

I rode out to meet Mordred on the day they reached the fort. Amhar, pale and grim, nodded to me and led the men on by, leaving us alone.

Mordred reached and touched my face, as if he did not quite believe in my presence.

"Nimiane," he said. "Nimiane. I heard you call, but there was no time. He wouldn't wait to talk. Nimiane, I've killed my brother."

I held him while he wept.

A council took place, loud and angry.

"We'll all be branded traitor for this treaty with Childriche," the young Duke of Cornwall shouted. "I said Mordred had no authority to make such a peace."

"You said no such thing in my hearing," Amhar roared, and he sounded so like Arthur in a temper that the hall fell silent.

"Gawain wasn't here," said Guenevere. "Arthur wasn't here. You were, Constantine. You know what we faced."

"If we hadn't made that peace, Childriche could have reached even to Cornwall," I said. "Hold your temper, Constantine. This may yet be resolved."

"Resolved? With Gawain dead?"

"Gawain isn't dead," I said.

Guenevere's look lightened. Mordred shook his head. We both knew his brother could not live, though he might linger even a week.

"Even if he does die, there was no treason but in his perception. The King knows Gawain to be rash and reck-less," Guenevere said. "This is misunderstanding, nothing more. I'll send a message to Arthur and set all straight."

"I don't think he'll take your word," I said, with a look at the Harper of Munster hovering behind her, faithful hound. I did not bother to apologize for the accusation. Guenevere only bowed her head. Her hand found mine, so that we sat like sisters, with the world breaking around us. The treaty with Childriche was no treason, only grim necessity, given our circumstances. The other thing ....

"Perhaps it is I who should go to Rome," said Mordred. "Nimiane?"

"I've always wanted to travel," said Amhar, to no-one in particular, and for a moment I wanted both to laugh and cry, as Mordred gave him a bleak look that spoke nonethe-less of returning life.

"I'll send messages to meet the King," Mordred said. "Gawain's return must mean Arthur's."

It was far too late. Arthur should have come to us when he was needed — or not at all. We could at least have lived in the peace we had made, preserved against the creeping Saxon tide.

I wrote a letter to the King. I said nothing of Guenevere's infidelities — that was between the two of them, and I could no more betray Mordred than cut out my own heart. Besides, Guenevere deserved better of me. She had, perhaps, deserved better of Arthur. In the past few years she had finally come to carry her authority well. A pity she had never been allowed it in the early wars, when added maturity in his wife might have held the King's heart, as beauty alone could not.

I told Arthur of the raids, of the Saxon armies, of Childriche's forces rolling over the east, a heathen wave. I reminded him of the numbers he had taken to Less Britain and thence to Rome, and of how we had had no word since Bedwyr's death and the beginning of his pilgrimage. We could not know his will, and we sought to preserve something of what his sword had won. I made clear that it was by my advice the Queen and Mordred had acted, and that they had done so with the full support of the kings and dukes of Britain. If we had done wrong I begged his mercy.

Mordred, I think, tried to assume all responsibility for the peace with Childriche, and swore he would set out for Rome himself, once the kingdom was returned to Arthur's keeping.

Guenevere wrote, but I do not know what she said.

Our messenger found the King at Gawain's deathbed. Arthur threw the parchments on the fire with the seals unbroken. Once Gawain was buried he came on.

I rode to meet the King's army myself, alone.

"Lady Nimiane," he greeted me. Not "cousin".

"My lord," I said, and bowed, as I do not think I ever had before. "It's good to see you back at last from Rome."

"I never reached Rome," he said. "I turned for Britain when I heard my nephew had assumed the crown."

"That, my lord, was a lie."

"Was it? In Brittany we heard he had dishonoured the Queen my wife, and we laughed. In Massilia it was said he had taken heathen allies, and no-one believed it. Below Florentia a messenger found me, sent on by Hoel. He said Mordred had granted lands in Britain to the Saxon Childriche."

"My lord, you must know how little choice we had."

"Gawain is dead."

"Gawain attacked Mordred as he patrolled the shore against Saxon landings. We have a treaty with Childriche; we do not trust him."

"Gawain died at Mordred's hand."

"No-one grieves for Gawain more than his brother. But my lord, you know Gawain. He attacked without warning and was beyond reach of all reason. And Mordred wishes for nothing other than that you return to govern your land again."

"What's left of it."

"Had we not dealt with Childriche there would have been nothing for you to return to. Nothing! Did you expect us to hold a kingdom against a people so populous with your name alone? My lord, we have done nothing that was not done in faith with you. Meet with Mordred. Talk to him. You'll see he doesn't desire your crown, and has never desired it. Trust me as you trusted my father."

"Your father wouldn't have betrayed me for love of an usurper."

"I betrayed no-one!" My hand shook on the reins, but my voice was steady. "My charge, as my father's, was ever Britain, not the King's person. Remember that before you call me traitor, who have been seven years gone from this land."

That shocked him almost as much as it shocked me. No-one had spoken so to Arthur since Merlin went.

"My lord, only meet with Mordred. Please." I bowed again and turned my horse for the fort.

"We will meet with the traitor," Cai called from Arthur's side. "But we will not come unarmed, remembering what happened in Vortigern's day."

Arthur said nothing at all, and I rode to the fort with the shadow on my heart growing darker, as though Fortune turned her face from us all alike, from Britain, as she had turned it from Rome.

We sat by my fire all that night, Mordred and Amhar and I. Guenevere left us, for her harper or her prayers. Constantine of Cornwall left us, too, and took his household men with him.

"Let them go," Mordred said, when a man came from the gate with that news. "We do not go to war in the morning."

The fire was dark, shadowed with the shapes of men and ravens.

"We should leave," I said. "We three, and the Queen. We should slip away like foxes in the night, and leave Arthur to reclaim what he can."

"I've done no wrong," Mordred said. "To Britain, I've done no wrong. But you and Amhar should go, put yourselves beyond reach of the King's anger. Take Guenevere to some safety."

"I'm not the one he mistakes for his enemy," the King's son said. "Take Nimiane away, Mordred. You and she can see the Queen to some refuge."

"If you both stay, I stay," I said. "Arthur is angry, not mad as Gawain was. In the morning we'll talk. Perhaps we three will go into exile together."

It seemed to me reasonable that it should be so, if the King could not forgive what we had done. Arthur was never unreasonable, never unjust, once his brief tempers passed. But the night held the cries of dying men; I could not understand it, and was afraid, with no means to turn the gathering tide. A little before dawn I rose and left the men. I went to the King's hall and woke Guenevere's harper. We found the Queen in the chapel lying before the altar, with the tears dried on her face.

"Take her away," I told the Munsterman. "Now, before the daybreak."

Guenevere got slowly to her feet, and in the dim light of the altar lamps she seemed faded, old.

"What of you, Nimiane?" was all she asked.

"I stay until the end," I said. "Whatever it may be."

"You don't know."

I shook my head. "I cannot see. But I do not think it will end well."

"I'll pray for us all," she said, and kissed me, before walking ahead of the harper from the chapel. It was the last time I saw her, save once, when I travelled to her abbey and found we had nothing left to say.

Then I went back to my own house, where the fire, untended, had died. Mordred, Amhar, and I sat shoulder to shoulder on the bench by the door, watching the eastern horizon for the dawn. We held hands like children against the dark, taking what comfort and strength we could from the contact, skin on warm skin.

the morning came, and we went to meet with Arthur.

The songs still tell of it, one way and another. We met afoot. The King's men watched, and ours. Arthur addressed us as one grieved by our errors, but he was willing to speak with us as he had not been the day before, willing to listen.

He did not speak of treason and I had hope, though young Constantine was at his side, never meeting my eyes.

Cai glowered. "We will be another generation undoing all this coward's peace."

"We are the last of Britain," I said then. "All you have left to hope for, Cai, are songs."

Arthur frowned us all to silence.

"Where is my queen?" he asked.

"Knowing the falsehoods that have blackened her name, I sent her to a place of safety," I said. That was the only time I ever lied to my King. "I feared for her, since in foreign lands some have learnt to trust the idle gossip of singers over the tried fidelity of friends."

"Saxons till fields in the east; I don't call that idle gossip. A Saxon calls himself king on British soil."

"What would you have had me do?" Mordred demanded. "Fight till the last of us were dead and the heathen poured inland? Would you rather have come home to find Childriche feasting in your hall and Guenevere serving in his bed? Look how few you left me with, to hold your land for seven years." And he waved a mailed fist around at the household warriors and the kings who still stood by us, massed behind on the hill.

Constantine shouted and drew his sword. I still do not know if it was deliberate provocation on his part, or honest error. Perhaps it was fear, the guilt of his own betrayal showing him treachery everywhere.

He won a kingdom by it, for the little time it endured.

Constantine flung himself before the King. Mordred drew in his own defence, shouting, "Amhar — Nimiane!"

Amhar plucked me from Constantine's wild path, dragged me to a horse. I heard Arthur shouting, "Hold! Peace!" but mounted warriors were rushing in, ours from the hill, his from behind. Both sides raised the cry of

Treachery, treachery. There was no survival on that field but by sword's edge.

Amhar left me in the shadow of the woods and rode, to Mordred or to his father, or only into the general madness.

So many died that day, true men, true to Arthur, true to Mordred. I saw them all. Old men, who had thought Briton would never fight Briton again. Boys I had seen grow to men, withstanding Saxon raids. Cai. Arthur, my King, my only King. Mordred, my brooding angel, who was friend, lover, dear as brother. Mordred.

They say they killed one another, he and the King. It is not true. Battle swept them apart — face to face, mounted, visible to all, they might still have stayed the fury. But they were washed into the milling madness afoot, and *traitor* was the word cried upon them both. They died. I wept, and cursed the fool Constantine, that he might come to know as we had there was no withstanding the shifting of the world.

It was he who had to treat with Childriche, when spring came again.

I haᴆ them ᴄᴀʀʀɪᴇᴆ ᴀᴡᴀʏ to the Ladies. I would not leave them for their graves to become shrines, or places of abhorrence. We left Arthur's name, for what strength it could lend to Constantine against the heathen.

Childriche was cautious, for a little, hearing rumours of the King's return. But Constantine was never blessed in his kingship, and his was an ill-fated line. Fate and Fortune stood against him, and the weight of Saxon armies.

I do not believe in curses, even mine.

Amhar lived, lamed and blind, to make songs in the orchard of Avalon over his father's grave, and his friend's. After a few seasons he began to smile once more, making lighter songs for our children.

A noRtheRn tiðe will come against the Saxons. They will make of us a story to give them heart, as they hold back the heathen raids and watch for longboats. They will lose their kingdom in the end, and dream of ours. But that is all to come. The British kings and the Saxon fight, and every year the warbands push further inland. We hold only the distant hills. Arthur already is a song and not a man, a name of glory on the wind.

Here, there is still a peaceful orchard, where Amhar lies now beside Mordred and Arthur the King.

Even this place will not endure against the driving Saxon wave.

When I lie between Mordred and Amhar under the orchard grass, my granddaughter's children, with their Roman-dark eyes, will go into the hills of the west.

anno domini
nine hundred and ninety-one
two voices

In this year Ipswich was harried, and very soon after that Byrhtnoth the Ealdorman was slain at Maldon.

I

DRIVE THE HORSES AWAY, we'll not be running from this fight. No retreat, no bridge to burn, no bridge to cross. The Danes have the island, beached ships behind them; we hold the bank across the Pante, the Blackwater.

Drive the horses away, we'll not be riding back to the mothers, the wives and the girls, not from this fight.

What a forlorn hope, to dare to stand against this rising tide. Always it comes, sweeping from the east, the north. Waves of folk. First the men, then the wives, the sons, the braid-crowned daughters.

The Romans came, and the British drank them, waves sinking into the sand. The Saxons came, and we overran the British, scattered the sands. What is Arthur now but a name in the wind?

Cerdic and Cynric, Hengist and Horsa, land of the Angle, land of the Saxon, land of the Frisian and Jute. Ebb tide for the house of Alfred in Aethelred the unfortunate. The weak, perhaps. A brother's murder can be difficult, though his was not the hand, nor his the will. A taint of blood to unsettle a bloody time. A misfortunate time.

Danish kings on an English throne: Swein, Knut, Harold, Harthaknut. This awaits us. And in the end the Confessor and a jumped-up bastard planted on other shores by other Norsemen.

Here we act as motif, foreshadow the fall of the line of Wessex.

Drive the horses away, cast the hawk to the woods and free her, draw up and wait. We cannot come at the raiders yet.

A few arrows fly. What if we fail?

They come on, harry, burn, seize. What they have done before, will do again. There are no others to oppose them, no other levies to muster.

What of the king?

It is advised he pay them tribute for peace. And next year, more. And the year after, still more. And then it will be lands, villages, towns.

They breed too many sons in the north. There will be no stopping them but by defeat. Theirs.

Make them fear the island's fame. Call forth a champion from the fogs and set a name to win respect. Arthur.

Alfred. Ironside. Turn them to Ireland, to Flanders. Let them raid Sicily and carve out kingdoms. Build Novgorod. Sail to Byzantium. Sail to Iceland, Greenland, Vinland, there's a thought. Found a kingdom for yourselves in Newfoundland. Are we less valiant than the Skraelings? A winter on the Rock worse than Greenland?

No, our fat, green pastures call you, as they called us. The age of heroes is past.

Then Byrhtnoth began there to draw up the warriors, rode and instructed, directed the men, how they ought to stand and hold that place, and bade that they hold their shields aright, firmly with hands, and never fear.

Was there ever a time of heroes, or were they always such, standing in the chill, waiting. Thinking of death and women waiting?

He across the water, Anlaf, Olaf, Tryggvi's son, he'll be a hero yet, in his own time, his own place. Find a crown yet, in Norway, and lose one. He'll be an Arthur, return awaited. What are we but his youthful training? "Olaf raided in Essex," that's us, that's all this waiting and fearing.

The Vikings send a spokesman. He stands on the shore, calls across the dark water. Sent to bargain, gold for their going. First he speaks for our lord alone, then to us, the common fighting men whose families wait, then to Byrhtnoth again. But the meaning is the same in his threefold speech. Gold for peace.

"... and this is better for you, that you buy off this battle with tribute, than that we thus bitter battle share ..."

Peace for how long? For now, and tomorrow, and the day after? How long can we buy off a pirate? And if we buy Olaf, can we buy the Dane?

Is peace for a fortnight worth our pride?

"... here stands a noble earl with his company, that wants to defend this homeland, Aethelred's country, the land of my prince, his folk, his earth. .... It seems to me too shameful that you should go to your ships with our payment, and without a fight, now that you have come thus far over our ground."

So then, we fight. Pride of Essex. Hero of the East Saxons. Byrhtnoth, ealdorman, noble man.

Pride was the sin of Lucifer, the sin of the Garden, pride in the self's own strength.

And still the river between us, and a casual, stinging arrow. The tide ebbs, the river's tide. We stir ourselves and watch the swimming causeway.

Wulfstan is sent to hold it, Aelfere and Maccus beside him, we behind, and the raiders advance. Cautious. Reaching spears. They cannot pass, not while we hold the ford. And so they ask safe passage over.

What are we, children at sport, nobles sparring? These are our fields, our homes, our people they march on.

Then the earl began in his pride to allow too much land to the hateful people.

We draw back. They cross unhindered, shrugging at cold water, minds ahead, stomachs tight as ours.

Only God knows who will be able to control the battlefield.

More glory to Him if we give up our little advantage? Or more glory to Byrhtnoth?

Like a wave they come, grey helms, grey mailed shoulders, grey spear-tips glint, dip, scramble, a wave rolling ashore from the island. No hope wet feet will slow them. Are their feet ever dry in their long, low ships?

We form the shield-wall, waiting.

They come, the carrion-seekers. Ravens. Eagles. It is said they can hear the jingle of mail, the clash of swords, for miles. Smell the slaughter on the slightest breeze. Or it may be they follow the heathen horde. They circle, calling, waiting. Beasts of the pagan gods.

The time was coming that fated men would fall there.

Come, come and have done with. Why do we wait?

II

THE SHOUT, THE ROAR reaching to heaven. The first launching of spears, the rushing flight, the cries. Stink of blood and ruptured bodies as we smash together.

There was an uproar on earth.

The named that fell, the named that did great deeds. Wulfmaer, sister's son to Byrhtnoth, cut down. Edward the Chamberlain slew his slayer, earned our lord's thanks.

What of the sister, the mother? An easy grant of too much land when we had them penned, and will she count the gesture worth the price?

She may at that. It was a bold death, a noble death. A hero's death, to be remembered. A tribute to his remembrance, no tribute paid.

After the nephew, the uncle. A Viking throws his spear and the earl is wounded. Byrhtnoth knocks spear from body with his shield, tears it free, and thrusts the same weapon back again. One moment's exultation, no more. The proud Viking dies on his own point. Another feels the ealdorman's anger.

Then the brave man laughed, gave thanks to the Creator for the day's work, that the Lord gave him.

Laugh and give thanks. A Viking lets fly a spear, a fated blow, and the earl is stricken, stumbling, falling. By his side a young man, another Wulfmaer. A boy, he is nothing but a velvet-jawed boy, and his mother would that she kept him home. He draws the spear from our lord, returns it with the strength of outraged youth, that his lord should fall with his men so close about him, who ought to shield his life.

Another Viking upon the earl. They are among us now, and he stoops, seeking plunder, bright gold of Byrhtnoth's arm-rings, gold of the ealdorman's sword. Too soon he gloried in another's conquest, that gold-greedy warrior, too soon thought he heard a soul summoned to heaven, to Valhalla, Saint Michael and the Martyr Edward, Valkyries escorting. Byrhtnoth draws sword, swings, and is prevented. Lifeless sword drops to earth. There are none to stand over him.

We are overrun.

"I thank Thee, Lord Ruler, for all the joys that I experienced in the world. Now, mild

CReaToR, I haoe greatest neeð, that Thou
grant my soul gooð, so that it to Thee might
traoel in Thy power, Lorð of Angels, to go
with peace. I am suppliant to Thee that the
hell-thieoes will not be able to harm it."

Eyes to heaven, no help on earth. No strength held in
reserve, no banners over the hill. None to stand over him?
None to guard the cooling soulless case from stripping
hands?

None living, none. All entangled in the myriad spinning
fights, hand to hand, man to man. Let the dead guard the
dead, loyal thegns lie with their lord, shielding him.

Then the heathen men heweð him anð both
the warriors that stooð by him, Aelfnoth
anð Wulfmaer, both lay ðeað then, alongsiðe
their lorð they gaoe up life.

III

AND HOW MANY OTHERS, dying along the shore? To fall by
your lord, there's a way to undying memory, eternal name.
If chance drags you off, then fall unnamed in other corners
of the field.

Still, it is better thus, to fall and be forgot in falling.
Better not to be remembered fleeing, reviled across the
ages.

Then they turneð away from battle, those
that ðið not want to be there.

Did any want to be there? We would rather be at home
with wives, with hounds, with cattle, tending to our fields.
Perhaps the thegns, the housecarls, the earl's sworn retain-

ers had come, battle-eager when summoned. Their duty is to fight, ours to defend our own.

Yes, they would come, eager for spoils, for glory. Byrhtnoth's men, his by right of fellowship, his by bread and mead and gifts of gold, by horses, hawks, and hounds. So a lord wins his men's hearts, and so their blood is owed him. Even after his fall.

Especially after his fall.

Ðere Oðða's sons were first in flight.

Godric, Godwine and Godwig. They fled, to their father's shame, their mother's dishonour, Godric riding the earl's horse. Some followed, seeing the earl retreat, thinking the day was done, not knowing he lay in the mud and the horse ran masterless under an oath-breaking thief.

... they ðið not care for war, but turned from the battle anð sought the wooðs, fleð to that fastness anð saveð their lives, anð many more with them than was fitting, if they then ðeserveð all the favours which he haò given to them as retainers.

But this is not an age of heroes, men do not live and die with their lords as they should. We know the Danes have bought faith and sold swords among the earls and the abbots and the bishops. It is whispered in every holding. Why else would they raid so unopposed?

Speak truth. We are a weak and ailing nation, our spirit sapped by blood, weak as Edward slumping from his saddle in the step-mother's yard. And wolves flock to the dying.

Call for a champion unfettered by conscience! Lend us Arthur, Hrolf, the Maccabees! Or can we stir up heart

among ourselves, are we yet men of honour, fit for freedom?

Then there went forth proud thegns,
undaunted men hastened eagerly; they all
wanted one of two things, to forsake life or
to avenge their beloved lord.

We rally, close our scattered ranks, draw breath. We
have not broken, not run. Fit, in the end, for lasting fame.
Let infamy ride with the sons of Odda; we who fall, even
the unnamed, earn here a hero's rest. And the named?
Let them resound through the centuries, men who
fought for honour, nothing more. Give them that; it takes
none from us, we who lie beside them. Aelfwine the young
Mercian, none will dare decry his share. He will not shame
his father, grandfather, not show his face among the lords
of Mercia to be told that he broke faith.

Then he went forth remembered to battle.

And his example spurs us all.

Then companions began to urge friends and
comrades, that they go forth.

Yes, give us noble speech, remind us why we fight
when hope is gone. The day will yet be theirs, and theirs the
shore. Free to ride inland, free to raid, no turning them now.
Perhaps some one will buy them off, this time, too late for
us. And yet we, we few, have greater virtue for a song. And
that is fame. And fame will give us noble speech.

Offa spoke, shook ash-spear:
"Lo thou, Aelfwine, hast urged all thegns
to danger, now that our lord lies there, the

earl on the earth. For us is it needful, that each encourage the other, warriors to battle, as long as he is able to have and hold weapons, the bitter blade, the spear and good sword. Odda's cowardly son Godric has betrayed us all by turning so very many men when he rode on that horse, on that proud horse as though he were our lord; therefore here on the field the folk was divided, the shield-wall broken. Damn him, that he here so many men put to flight!"

Leofsunu, too, brandishing spear, recalls a vow that he would never flee battle. Now he betters it, swears to advance seeking vengeance for the death of his lord. He, too, will have no word of derision carried to his home, he will never wander lordless in dishonour. Would his wife ask him back, beseech him to run to her, walk proudly under the shame, having her man still by her side? She has his honour, stark in verse.

He full of anger advanced, fought steadfastly, flight he scorned.

And what of us, we who elect to stay, caught by comrades' eyes, by women's shame, by pride or lack of chance?

Then Dunmere spoke, a humble freeman, brandished spear, shouted over all and bade that each warrior avenge Byrhtnoth:
"He who thinks to avenge our lord on this folk cannot draw back, nor care about fear."

Yes, we also, moved for honour, glory, vengeance, we advanced. What more to tell? The fight was bitter. All lost: brave, grand, gesturing lord, the battle, coastal homes, all.

Salvage some sense of worth and pray the women seek the woods.

But could we not have barred the ford?

And so we fight, and fall. Ashferth, a Northumbrian far from home, from kin, at stranger's hearth to seal a peace, he will bring no dishonour to his kin when the news is taken home. Edward the Tall, rushing the Viking shieldwall, wreaking havoc in their lines, and Aetheric. And more, and more.

Shield-rims burst and the byrnie sang some terrible song.

Offa is dead, the bold maker of speeches, dead and mangled in the dirt. But take heed, all, he kept his vows; he died beside his friend, his lord.

We have vowed nothing, no mead-hall boasts bind us here. Yet see where we stand and die beside them. Recall, it is our herds and homes that they defend, beside their own.

Then were shields broken.

Wistan fought there, Oswold and Eadwold, Godric, Aethelgar's son ...

That was not the Godric that fled from the battle ...

Let that stand for us all. One battle lost among so many lost and won. Who wins in the end? *William?*

Let it be. We will fight the ground over again and again, feed it with our bones, guard it with our ghosts.

What do we leave that any recall? What prize in all this when it has been forgotten, was victory ours or no, did our wives sleep safe that night, were the Hours kept undisturbed?

Only this, old Byrhtwold's saying, only this to set against the terror and the horror and the glory of the day:

"Thought must be the sterner, hearts the keener, courage the greater, as our strength lessens."

This, this we leave. The ealdorman, the thegns, the churls, this is all that remains. Victory denied, defeat forgotten. Who will remember or care, once the women have wept and the monks have recorded? How many unnamed, with the few now recalled?

In the dust, it does not matter.

What is a hero in the end but a man a poet sang?

And in that year someone first advised that tribute be yielded to the Danish men, because of the great terror that they wrought by the coast. That was, at first, ten thousand pounds.

about the author

k.v. johansen is the author of a number of fantasy and science fiction novels for children and teens, including *Nightwalker*, which received the 2008 Ann Connor Brimer Award for outstanding contribution to children's literature in Atlantic Canada and was on VOYA's Best Science Fiction, Fantasy and Horror list in 2007, and *Torrie and the Pirate-Queen*, winner of the 2006 Lilla Stirling Award from the Canadian Authors' Association. Both *Nightwalker* and *Torrie and the Firebird* were on the Ontario Library Association's top ten "best bets" for children lists in 2007 and 2006 respectively. She has Master's Degrees in Medieval Studies (Centre for Medieval Studies, Toronto) and in English (McMaster). Her main scholarly interests are medieval and ancient history and languages, but she held the 2001 Eileen Wallace Research Fellowship in Children's Literature from the Eileen Wallace Collection at the University of New Brunswick while working on *Quests and Kingdoms: A Grown-Up's Guide to Children's Fantasy Literature*, which was nominated for the 2006 Harvey Darton Award in the UK, and her work on recent Canadian children's fantasy, published as *Beyond Window-Dressing; Canadian Children's Fantasy at the Millennium*, received the 2004 Frances E. Russell Award from the Canadian branch of IBBY, the International Board on Books for Young People.

Johansen's website is at: www.pippin.ca

Other books published by Sybertooth Inc.
www.sybertooth.ca

~~~~~~

The Canvas Barricade
by Donald Jack

In print for the first time, Donald Jack's comedy *The Canvas Barricade* was the first modern play performed on the main stage of the Stratford Festival (1961).

Misty Woodenbridge, a painter, has rejected the materialism of modern society for life in a tent by the Ottawa River, where he lives as carefree as the fabled grasshopper, eating stolen apples and painting masterpieces. But as summer draws to an end, reality rears its ugly head, and Misty must choose between starving in his tent and moving to the city with his fiancée. Meanwhile, his in-laws-to-be smell a cash cow when a mysterious art buyer begins snapping up Misty's work – and naturally they keep the money. Out of kind consideration for Misty's artistic ideals, of course...

ISBN-10: 0968802494 • ISBN-13: 9780968802496
Trade paperback • published 2007
£12.00 • $16.00

~~~~~~

Other books published by Sybertooth Inc.
www.sybertooth.ca

~~~~~~

QUESTS AND KINGDOMS
A Grown-Up's Guide to Children's Fantasy Literature
By K.V. Johansen

An historical survey of children's fantasy literature for the inter-ested general reader, of great practical value to library and educa-tion professionals as well. For those who already know and love the classics of children's fantasy, *Quests* will be an introduction to works and authors they may have missed.

Praise for *Quests and Kingdoms*

"...exceptionally well written and recommended for its relevance for teachers and or parents..." -**Midwest Book Review**

"...this is not only a fine reference tool but a finely-written book...This is undoubtedly a seminal work guaranteed to stimulate discussion on children's literature..." -**Books in Canada**

"I can think across the years of Marcus Crouch and Sheila Egoff, Neil Philip and Colin Manlove, Jack Zipes and Humphrey Car-penter, and J.R.R. Tolkien himself .... Johansen's *Quests and Kingdoms* is a welcome newcomer to this critical tradition."
-Children's Books History Society Newsletter

ISBN-10: 0968802443 • ISBN-13: 9780968802441
462pp • $30.00 • £20.00 • Trade paperback

~~~~~~

Other books published by Sybertooth Inc.
www.sybertooth.ca

~~~~~~

Donald Jack's classic, triple Leacock Medal winning
historical fiction series, *The Bandy Papers*

It's Me Again: Volume III of The Bandy Papers
ISBN-10: 097395051X • ISBN-13: 9780973950519
Trade paperback • published 2007
£12.00 • $16.00
Me Bandy, You Cissie: Volume IV of The Bandy Papers
ISBN-10: 0973950579 • ISBN-13: 9780973950571
Trade paperback • published 2008
£12.00 • $16.00
This One's On Me: Volume VI of The Bandy Papers
ISBN-10: 0973950552 • ISBN-13: 9780973950557
Trade paperback • published 2008
£12.00 • $16.00
Me So Far: Volume VII of The Bandy Papers
ISBN: 9780973950502
Trade paperback • published 2007
£12.00 • $16.00
Hitler Versus Me: Volume VIII of the Bandy Papers
(includes the novelette 'Where Did Rafe Madison Go?')
ISBN-10: 0968802486 • ISBN-13: 9780968802489
Trade paperback • published 2006
£12.00 • $16.00
Stalin Versus Me: Volume IX of The Bandy Papers
ISBN-10: 0968802478 • ISBN-13: 9780968802472
Trade paperback • published 2005
£11.00 • $16.00

~~~~~~

Sporeville : Volume I of *The Wellborn Conspiracy*
By Paul Marlowe

A darkly humorous steampunk mystery set in the 1880s, featuring a séance, a girl who is part werewolf, and a Confederate eugenicist with an army of sleepwalkers....

"...It was absolutely the best, most delicious thing I have read in some time." - Bonnie Campbell, *Resource Links*

Ages 12+ • ISBN-13: 9780973950540 • $10.95 / £6.95

...and in Fall 2008, the sequel: *Knights of the Sea*
Volume II of *The Wellborn Conspiracy*

The Drone War
A *Cassandra Virus* Novel
By K.V. Johansen

Jordan O'Blenis may be a genius when it comes to computers, but with spies after his sister's research in unmanned aerial vehicles, he needs all the help he can get from Cassandra, an artificial intelligence inhabiting the web, to keep her safe and to save BWB Aerospace's top secret drone project.

Ages 9+ • ISBN-13: 9780973950526
$9.95 / £5.95

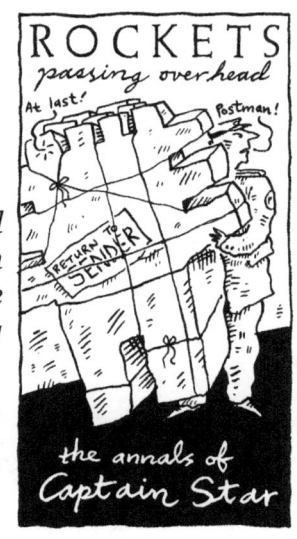

And coming soon, the first collected edition of Steven Appleby's Captain Star comic strips, which were the basis for a TV cartoon starring Richard E. Grant as Captain Star.

More on the book at:
www.captainstar.net

www.ingramcontent.com/pod-product-compliance
Lightning Source LLC
Chambersburg PA
CBHW060753180626
46818CB00002B/559